THE
EXTORTIONERS

Also by John Creasey

THE THEFT OF THE MAGNA CARTA
A SPLINTER OF GLASS
INSPECTOR WEST TAKES CHARGE
INSPECTOR WEST AT HOME
ALIBI

THE EXTORTIONERS

by

JOHN CREASEY

Charles Scribner's Sons
New York

Printed in the United States of America
Library of Congress Catalog Card Number 74–14013
ISBN 0–684–13927–8

1

Rich Man

"You're a rich man," said the stranger on the telephone. "You can pay twenty thousand pounds without missing it. Don't make any mistake, Clayton. You pay the money or your wife knows about your little peccadillo." The speaker gave a curiously mirthless laugh. "If that's what you like to call it."

He fell silent, but Oliver Clayton did not speak.

"Are you there?" the caller asked, sharply. "I'm not fooling. I can give her chapter and verse, going back over nineteen years. I can tell her *every*thing. To keep those secrets, twenty thousand pounds is cheap."

Still Clayton did not speak.

"Answer me!" the speaker rasped. "You're still there, I can hear you breathing. Answer me!"

Very slowly and deliberately, Clayton put down the receiver.

He was at the large, pedestal desk in a spacious, book-lined room; both spacious and gracious. French windows opened onto a narrow lawn and a herbaceous border not yet in full colour, for it was early spring; but there were crocuses and daffodils and some flowering shrubs, vivid in the afternoon sun. Morning rain had given the green fresh brightness and the flowers clarity of colour. Sparrows flew and a robin pecked at a patch of ground newly dug by Rosamund.

1

By his wife.

It was a bright and beautiful afternoon; and this room was full of light. Yet it also seemed full of shadows; near darkness; menace. The weathered red brick wall, with its ramblers—tied and trained by Rosamund—already in leaf, gave a sense of solidity to the tranquility out there, but in his heart and mind there was the beginning of awful turbulence.

Fear.

He had a mind which scholars conceded was as lucid as a man's could be but just now it was clouded; even thoughts would not come, only the fears. He felt as if he had come up against some dark, forbidding, unyielding mass which spread pain throughout his body and along his limbs.

He did not—yet—ask himself who could possibly know of his other life.

He sat back in his padded swivel chair, with the high back against which he rested his dark head; a pale patch showed where the hair was going thin. He had a long, narrow face, with sensitive lips and a sensitive nose, dark, deepset, very bright eyes. Their present brightness was caused by pain. His long, slender hands gripped the arms of the chair as if some hidden compulsion put power into him.

Slowly, he relaxed.

In a voice little above a whisper, he said: "Oh, dear God."

He shivered.

There was no sound in the room but his breathing, none outside except the hum of a car, moving along this quiet street in Hampstead. Beyond the garden he could see the tops of beech trees on the Heath, beyond the trees the high, white cloud and the clear blue sky.

He moistened his lips, and said again: "Oh, dear God."

When at last he focussed his eyes, it was on a photograph of Rosamund and the two girls, when they had been young; Angela, ten, Bertha, eight. An age ago. Both were married now, Angela had a child of her own, and only occasionally was this big

2

house filled with people or with voices, with footsteps or with laughter. There was just Rosamund and himself.

Just Rosamund.

Here, he had grown into the habit of forgetting—yes, forgetting!—his other life.

Forgetting?

Perhaps more truly he had become able over the years to put it out of his mind, emotionally, when he was here; to live, behave, think, as if Ida and her son—their son—did not exist, or, if they were alive, existed in a different world which had nothing to do with this one.

At last, he was beginning to think a little, and the obvious question came: what should he do?

Out of the blue, the telephone call had come; out of the blue, a demand for twenty thousand pounds; out of the blue, the crashing of this part of his life, perhaps of all of his life.

What would Rosamund do, if she found out?

What would I do?

What of the children; the girls and their husbands, and: Kevin.

My *God!* What had been going on in his mind all these years? Had he really believed that the truth would never out? Had he lived in security for so long that he had lulled himself into believing that the security was true, not false?

He was sweating; at forehead and neck, lips and eyes; he was hot and cold.

What should he do?

Pay the man off?

Some inner voice answered: No. He did not listen at first, did not really hear it, for another thought came like the slash of a knife: he must not let Rosamund come back and find him like this. She would see at a glance that something was seriously wrong, and ply him with questions. He could not lie to her now, he had to get away, perhaps for a day or two, so that he could think clearly and make up his mind what to do. He glanced at a wall-clock, the ticking of which was so soft he could not hear a sound. It was twenty to four. Rosamund had gone to one of her do-gooding committees and the afternoon ones always spilled over into tea and cakes or tea and biscuits; she wouldn't be back until five o'clock, possibly half-past five to six.

He pushed his chair back and stood up—and the telephone bell rang.

The last time it had rung, he had not the faintest premonition of what the call would be about; it might have been from any one of a dozen, a hundred people, from a newspaperman to a tradesman, from a friend to a casual acquaintance. It had been the man with the husky voice, who had begun by asking:

"Is that Professor Clayton?"

"Yes," Oliver Clayton had answered.

"You won't know me, Professor," the man had said, "but I know a great deal about you."

In the light of what had followed that had been a sinister remark but at the moment Clayton had thought nothing of it. A dozen people might telephone or write and say much the same thing. He was a professor of zoology, who had worked for many years on tracing, through fossils found in mountains and sea beds, in underground oil masses and in countless mines in a hundred countries, the origin of animals. He had never set out with any specific purpose or objective in mind; just to explore, for his was a nature which throve on facts. He had written dozens of papers, all of which had appeared in obscure magazines throughout the world, some translated into over twenty languages, and he was an expert in a subject which few people considered of any great importance. Moreover, he was wealthy by inheritance, and could afford to do exactly what he wanted; and he wanted to investigate the history of mammals.

He had travelled widely, and in the early years, Rosamund had not been able to go with him. It was on one of his

4

expeditions, in Australia, that he had met Ida, and she had fallen in love with him.

And he, with her?

It had been very different from his first burning passion for Rosamund, and yet had not been simply physical. In fact Ida had looked after his creature comforts rather more than his sexual appetite. Yet he could remember the time when they had first lain together, in a shack beside a billabong in South Australia. A series of accidents had left them on their own, and Ida, a young student interested in fossils, had come along at least as much as cook and general help than for digging and research. She had been a pretty thing, with a nice figure, perhaps too heavy-breasted, and with beautiful grey eyes. He had woken on a Sunday morning to find her squatting close to him, those grey eyes close to him, smiling.

"My," she had said. "You look good enough to eat."

"And you," he had retorted, "look good enough to bed."

"Maybe I am," she had said. "Like to try me?"

Afterwards there had been such a vivid picture of Rosamund and the children in his mind; and, carelessly, he had left the photograph he had of them out, by the oddments of shaving and washing gear, so that when they had come back from the cave, chipping away at the rock and getting a good haul of sea-animal fossils as well as a few opals, Ida had picked it up and then looked at him.

"May I take a dekko, Professor?"

"Are you sure you want to?"

"Sure I'm sure."

"Then look," he agreed.

She had studied Rosamund for a long time. He had wondered what had been passing through her mind, wondered whether she would be resentful, or indifferent; whether she was falling in love with him, whether hurt for her was inevitable. Suddenly, she closed the leather case slowly, and said:

5

"They're a pair of beaut kids, Professor."

"They are, yes."

"And she's got everything it takes."

"Yes," he had answered.

"You in love with her?" Ida had challenged, and he had not hesitated to answer even though the words had come out slowly:

"In my way, yes."

"What's your way, Professor?" Ida had demanded. "Out of sight, out of mind? What the eye doesn't see the heart doesn't grieve about?"

To this day he could recall the hard, near-truculent tone and manner; remembered that he had realised in those moments that she *was* in love with him, that the morning's passion had not simply been a snatch at a passing mood.

"No," he had said.

"So you've got another way, all your own."

"I know what I feel and what I think," he had replied.

"Tell me, Professor, how do you feel and how do you think?"

Sitting on a wool-stuffed cushion with his back against a rock he had looked at her for a long time, very steadily; he could not remember any of the exact words, of course, but he could recapture the moods and be almost sure of the words. He had sensed the way her heart was beating, sense her yearning.

"I can love her," he said. "And love you."

"You mean you'd like a harem?" she had sneered.

"Ida," he had said, "it's very rare that one woman can give everything one man needs; equally rare the other way round. Society forces us to make-do. We settle for a lot of unhappiness and self-denial. I'm not making any proposals to you, I'm just telling you what I feel and what I think. I could be with you much of the time and not feel in the slightest degree disloyal to Rosamund, and with Rosamund without feeling the slightest sense of disloyalty to you. What I don't think—" He had broken off; even now, his lips twisted in the kind of wry smile which had twisted them so long ago.

6

"Well?" How her eyes had glowed in the evening sun. "What don't you think?"

"That you could be happy if you knew I was with her, or she would be happy if she knew about you."

"Too bloody right she wouldn't," Ida had said, almost viciously.

But that night she had come to him, and said: "I don't think I would mind, Professor."

"You need to be sure," he had replied.

"I've always wanted to come to England," she had said. "She—she wouldn't have to know about me. And you wouldn't have to keep me, either, I can work. I'm not going to be any bloody pommie's fancy girl!"

He had known it was crazy, but he had brought her back, and persuaded her to let him buy a flat for her in Bloomsbury, near the British Museum. She lived in the same flat now. Their son, Kevin, had been brought up in the flat. She had registered the child's birth, using her own name as his, saying she was a widow. She had taken an allowance from Oliver for him, but sent him to a Council school, then to one in Westminster. Now he was at London University, sharing rooms with another lad. To Kevin, Oliver was 'Uncle Oliver'. There was no way of being sure but Oliver believed Ida had been happy most of the time. He was certain that she had had some tempestuous affairs, and God knew he could not blame her. After the first, he had not really been jealous. The last had been some years ago.

Two lives.

It was a miracle that he had been able to keep them so separate that neither intruded on the other at all; had not until now.

A question began to thunder in his brain, driving out the thoughts of yesterday, all the nostalgia, even the more urgent fears.

"What am I going to do?" he asked himself aloud. *"What am I going to do? What am I going to do?"*

He could pay the blackmailer his twenty thousand pounds, but the 'no' was more insistent and so more audible and rational. There was no way of being sure the first demand would be the last. Much more likely there would be others, each more difficult to resist than those that had gone before. He *could* pay the blackmailer off but he must not.

He could tell Ida, and afterwards Rosamund.

He felt absolutely certain that once Rosamund knew he would have to break with Ida, or leave Rosamund, which would mean a divorce. *He did not want a divorce.* The simple truth was that he did not want to change his way of life at all. The years, if not the law, tied him as closely to Ida as to Rosamund, but they were such different women. He could not be sure how Ida would react but had some idea. After the first shock she would say:

"Well, it had to end one day, Professor, and we had a good run."

Nineteen, nearly twenty *years*. A good run!

She would probably add: "Kevin doesn't know you're his father, that's one good thing."

Good thing? his mind echoed. Was it so good? He had two daughters and a son and the son had never been acknowledged.

Only now, when the full truth was likely to break, was the enormity of the past attacking him with full force. My God! He couldn't deny the boy forever!

What should he do?

He could tell Rosamund, he reminded himself, but—what could she do, but ask him, expect him, to give Ida up? Either that, or divorce him. It was so much the convention. Not only she herself but her family, probably their daughters, would feel this was essential. He did not think it would make any difference which way he twisted and turned; if he told Rosamund the truth he would lose one life or the other.

What a bloody selfish fool!

What of the hurt this would cause Rosamund? How cold-blooded could one get, to think solely in terms of oneself? It was unthinkable to tell her that for practically all of their married life he had been decieving her. Divorce or no divorce, she would hang her head because of his shame.

He couldn't tell her; couldn't hurt her.

But what *could* he do?

Suddenly, swiftly, a thought came: the complete answer to his question and in that moment wholly complete and absolutely satisfying: so satisfying that he actually relaxed and smiled.

He could find his blackmailer, and kill him.

That way, no one need ever know; not Rosamund, not Ida; no one in the wide, wide world.

It was while the thought hovered in his mind that the telephone bell rang.

That was about the time when Sir Douglas Fellowes, a civil servant in a position of good standing and great trust at Whitehall, sat at his opulent desk in his opulent office, with a pen in his hand and a single sheet of paper in front of him. His expression was set and stern, the only muscles which moved were those at his jaws, and they very slowly.

At last, he put the broad gold nib to paper, and in a bold, flowing hand which did not tremble he wrote:

I want it to be clearly understood that the reasons I have for taking my life are purely personal. Nothing even remotely connected with my post in Her Majesty's Civil Service, is at stake.

He lifted the pen from the paper and stared at the tall window opposite the desk; for the first time, his lips were unsteady, but his hand was not as he began to write again.

I have every reason to believe that I have cancer of the most malignant kind. This is my one and only reason for what I am about to do.

He raised his hand again, hesitated, and then appended his signature as he had many thousands, perhaps hundreds of thousands of times, in his distinguished career.

2

The Demand

Oliver Clayton stared at the black instrument on the desk. It quivered slightly as it rang, but for a few moments he could not bring himself to lift it. Then he thought: it might be the blackmailer! and snatched up the telephone, but raised it more slowly to his ear. His voice was hoarse as he said:

"This is Professor Clayton."

"Don't ring off on me again," said the caller.

Clayton gulped, but didn't speak. It was not because he would not, but because for a few seconds he could hardly breathe and so could not find words. The silence everywhere else seemed deeper and more profound.

"Do you hear me?" the other rasped.

"Yes," Clayton answered at last.

"Don't ring off, and don't try any tricks. You know what I want."

"I—I know," Clayton acknowledged.

"Twenty thousand pounds."

"Yes."

"Tomorrow, at noon."

"I—I can't," Clayton made himself say.

"You'd better, or I'll be on the telephone to your wife."

"I've—I've an important conference at eleven o'clock in the morning," explained Clayton. "If I'm not on time there'll be a hue and cry. It's got to be a different time."

"Oh," the blackmailer said, as if taken by surprise, and rather weakly he asked: "What conference?"

"At the British Museum."

"About those old fossils?"

"I—yes. Yes, that's right."

"What time does the conference finish?"

"It could go on through the afternoon, until—"

"I must have that money tomorrow!" the blackmailer interrupted.

Clayton did not know when the change in his own attitude had started; when the black despair lifted and he began to be sensitive to things apart from the stark fact of the blackmail demand. But he detected a false, or at least a strange note in the man's voice and in that harsh insistence: "I must have that money tomorrow!" This gave to Clayton, with his clear and clinical mind, a feeling that he was not wholly on the defensive even on the telephone.

He said: "Well, you can't have it."

"I must!"

"Don't be absurd," said Clayton. "My bank—my main bank—is in Holborn. It doesn't open until ten o'clock and at that time in the morning I would need an hour to get there from here. Traffic is almost impossible. And—"

"You cut the conference," interrupted the other.

"Then everyone will start checking on me," retorted Clayton. "The Secretary of the British Museum will telephone my wife and she will have to report that I left earlier than usual. They'd assume something was wrong, and before you knew where you were the police would be looking for me."

The man interrupted in a savage slash of words: "If you go to the police you won't have a chance!"

"If I don't go to that conference the police will turn London upside down for me," retorted Clayton, and now he was revelling in his ascendancy, and the other's anxiety about getting the money the next day seemed to become more and

12

more strange. "It's an annual meeting and specialists from all over the world will attend. I've never missed or been late for one in my life."

He left the word 'life' hanging, and did not go on.

"You could send a message—"

"Well, I won't," Clayton stated.

There was silence for what seemed a long time. He could hear the other breathing, and thought: he has a cold or he's just getting over one. That shadow of despair had completely lifted, but unease was creeping into his brief mood of triumph, spoiling the elation he had felt when he had first thought of killing this man.

He was not a killer.

At last, the blackmailer said in a complaining voice: "There's nothing to stop you from getting the money at ten o'clock, and keeping it with you all day."

"Oh, use your head!" protested Clayton, sharply. "There's every reason. I can't go to the bank and take out twenty thousand pounds without telling them in advance, and they'd have to know why I wanted it."

"It's no business of theirs!"

"I couldn't stop them from wondering, and asking."

"Professor," the man said, in a high-pitched voice, "you're making difficulties for the sake of them. *Don't.* I want that money tomorrow and I mean to have it."

Clayton took what he knew to be a wild chance when he replied, and with an unmistakable note of asperity he said:

"Well, you will not get it from me."

He actually began to ring off, but some invisible force stopped him. The snuffling breathing of the man at the other end of the line seemed louder, and the actual breaths seemed more shallow, as if he were labouring under the stress of a great emotion. Clayton held on, his fingers very tight about the receiver, actually painful because of the tension.

He heard a door bang, and on the instant thought: Rosa-

13

mund's back! Then in a new panic he thought: she mustn't come in here, she mustn't hear what I'm saying. He had a wild impulse to bang the receiver down; another, to get up and lock the door. Slowly, the beating of his heart steadied and he reminded himself that she seldom did come in here during the day, respecting his need to concentrate too much. But he was sweating again and knew that he was very pale; if by chance she did come in she would need no telling that something was wrong.

The other man said: "Listen to me, Clayton," and when Clayton didn't reply at once he asked in a rising voice: "Are you there?"

"Yes, I'm here." Clayton was glad that his voice kept steady; there seemed to be two sides to him, the one who was sensitive to all the dangers and the fears, and the one who responded as if nothing about this really frightened him.

"Tomorrow is Tuesday."

"I know."

"I want the money on Wednesday."

"I can get it by then," Clayton said.

"Are you sure?"

"Yes. There's no morning session of the conference, only small meetings. I can go to the bank in the morning."

"You go. And you get it. Understand?"

Clayton said, suddenly weary: "All right, I'll get it."

"You get it, in five pound notes—not tens or anything high. And put it in a carrier bag. A brown paper shopping bag. Is that clear?"

Stiffly, Clayton said: "Yes."

"And take it to the Strand Corner House—do you know where I mean?"

"Yes," Clayton answered.

"Leave it at the cloakroom on the floor where the Carvery Restaurant is, and the Grill and Cheese. Leave it in the name of Higginbottom. Is *that* clear?"

14

Almost stifled, Clayton said again: "Yes, it's clear."

"Be there at a quarter to one, and leave it, and go away," the other ordered. "Just leave the bag and go away. You'll be under surveillance, and if you do anything you shouldn't, if you disobey in the slightest detail, then by God you'll be in trouble!"

Clayton said: "I understand."

"Mind you do what I say."

"I'll do it."

The man at the other end of the line rang off; the noise stung Clayton's ear. He put his receiver down slowly, then sank back in his chair. He could hardly believe his own mood of submissiveness but he knew what had brought it about. In the first place, realisation and acceptance of the fact that his thought of killing the other man had been a kind of bravado; a puff-up of courage which he had needed for a while but had soon gone. In the second place, Rosamund was home.

He saw her in the garden.

She carried a garden basket and some secateurs, and wore a scarf loosely around her head and a woollen cardigan draped about her shoulders; the empty sleeves dangled. She was going to cut flowers for the house, and went first to a thick bed of daffodils, there for cutting; he watched her as she went down on one knee, brown, knee-length skirt like a fan about her legs. A robin appeared, close to her, and she paused to talk to it, and he could see her smiling. His blood went cold. Soon, she was snipping and the robin was hopping near her while he, Clayton, shifted his chair so that he could not see Rosamund and so could not be seen if she turned round.

It would be difficult enough to compose himself to be with her for a drink before dinner; and during dinner. Somehow he would have to. He got up and went to one of the book-lined walls, taking down the *Naked Ape* without feeling his usual exasperation, even anger, with Desmond Morris for writing it. To him, it rang so false. He did not even thumb the pages, but stared at the rows of books. His mind was in a state of such confusion that he did not really try to think, just let one impression and one mood follow another.

And one contradiction followed another.

He could not allow Rosamund to know the truth; but it would be madness to pay blackmail.

He could never summon up enough courage to seek out and kill the blackmailer and yet he *must* kill the man. How else could he overcome the threat?

He could not go calmly to the bank in the morning—no, Wednesday morning—and draw out twenty thousand pounds; he had never drawn out more than a few hundred pounds in cash at one time before. Yet he had to draw it out if he were to do what he was told.

He must not pay the money over; but how else could he gain time?

He had gained twenty-four hours, but that was all—and twenty-four hours was nothing.

He drew his hand across his still damp forehead, feeling a touch of nausea. He had a headache, too, a tightness across the back of his eyes and his forehead, and pain at the back. That came from shock, of course; two hours ago he had never suspected blackmail. Two hours ago he had been living comfortably in this, the real centre of his life, with no thought of danger to it; and now the comfort, the love, the affection, were going to be torn asunder.

He thought: I *can't* talk to Rosamund about it. And he thought: I can't face dinner with Rosamund tonight. Almost as a revelation, he thought: *"I could talk to Ida!"*

He went back to his chair. Rosamund was no longer in the garden; she would be in the living-room or the dining-room, arranging the daffodils. It was no use, he couldn't calmly announce that he was going out, he would have to get through the early part of the evening with her somehow. It was already five o'clock, it would soon be time for the evening drink. He had grown into the habit of an early drink with Rosamund followed

16

by a bath and change before dinner at seven o'clock, because the cook-general had to be finished with everything, including the washing-up, by eight-thirty.

The telephone bell rang.

So complete was his absorption in himself that it made him jump; and then his heart began to thump, sickeningly, and he felt afraid to answer, in case it was the blackmailer. Savagely, he said aloud: "Supposing it is, what more can he do?" and he snatched up the receiver and barked: "Professor Clayton."

Ida said: "Oliver, I'm sorry to call you but I just had to."

Ida so seldom called.

He had known months pass without a call from her, she seemed to be content to wait for him. She worked part-time with a prominent travel agency—in fact her time was really her own for she had a circle of clients on whom she concentrated. Only when Kevin had been ill or she had been harassed or troubled had she telephoned him. There was the familiar note of apology in her voice and a note of desperation, too; a hint of fear. He had to make the call sound welcome, had to school himself to say:

"But of course, my sweet! It's always good to hear you."

"Oliver," she said. "Kevin's gone."

"Gone," he echoed.

"He's left home," she said flatly. "We—we had a terrible quarrel last night, and he went off on his motor-bike. I thought he'd come back. I was with some clients this afternoon, I've only just got back, and—and he's collected his clothes and everything, his room's stripped." Obviously she was fighting against tears. "I simply don't know what to do. I really don't."

Clayton said the only thing he possibly could: "I'll come and see you."

"Oh, can you?"

"Yes, of course." His mind was working with those quick flashes, and he saw one advantage: that he would now have to find an excuse for going out, for not having dinner with Rosamund. "Have you any idea where he might have gone?"

"Absolutely none," she replied, helplessly. "It was the last thing I expected. I—Oliver, what time can you come?"

"As soon as I've had time to change and get the car out," he said. "Will that be soon enough?"

"Yes," Ida said in a muffled voice, and she added: "Oh, bless you."

He replaced the receiver very slowly, and stood up at the same time. It was such a new development that momentarily at least it took his mind off his more urgent problem—good lord! What a time for this to happen! He straightened his desk and then went out of the study, which opened onto a passage alongside the stairs. The domestic quarters were at the end of this passage, the dining-room was on the other side of the staircase, opposite the study. If he guessed right Rosamund would be in a little scullery near the garden, arranging the flowers.

He had to tell her; there was no time for dithering, and so no time for nerves. He opened two doors, walked along a narrow stone-floored passage, past the open kitchen door and into the scullery, the door of which also stood wide open.

Rosamund was just coming in from the garden.

She still had the cardigan draped carelessly over her shoulders, and carried the flower basket, which had not only the daffodils but some early tulips and some sprays of flowering currant. She had been watching something which had obviously given her great pleasure, and her eyes were glowing, her cheeks as well, her lips were parted in a smile. At that first glimpse he thought, as he had thought a thousand times before, that she was the most beautiful woman he knew.

And at sight of him her eyes lit up even more; as if there were nothing she wanted so much as to see him approaching. And she had caught the evening sun in her corn-coloured hair and in those hazel brown eyes . . .

Chief Superintendent Roger West, of the Criminal Investigation Department at New Scotland Yard, was undergoing a rare experience; he was at his desk with no particular assignment on hand. He looked bronzed and magnificently fit, and as he grew older—he was in his mid-forties—he became more than ever worthy of the old soubriquet 'Handsome'. In fact he looked a little too good to be true as he ran through reports of cases which had been dealt with at the Yard while he had been on a three weeks' holiday—actually a holiday with his wife!—in South Africa, as a guest of a leading South African policeman. He had been at the Yard all day and the telephone had hardly rung, only half-a-dozen people had looked in to welcome him back. So when the telephone did ring, he started; but the receiver was in position in a flash.

"West," he announced.

"If you're not too busy, Handsome," a man said with overtones which oozed sarcasm, "come and see me, will you? I've a nice simple little investigation for you." The speaker was Commander Coppell of the C.I.D., Roger's immediate superior. "Ever heard of Sir Douglas Fellowes?"

Fellowes, Fellowes, Fellowes—ah!

"The Common Market specialist," he said.

"He used to be," replied Coppell. "He isn't any longer, he just killed himself. You mustn't go away so long again," he added with the same sarcasm. "This is the third V.I.P. suicide we've had in the last three weeks. So far, we don't know whether they're connected or coincidental. How long will you be?"

"Two minutes, sir," answered Roger, already out of his chair.

3

Rosamund

"Hullo, darling!" Rosamund welcomed Oliver Clayton. "Are you coming out for a breath of fresh air? It's lovely after the rain."

"I wish I were," he replied, with a grimace which he hoped seemed natural. "I came out to tell you I'm going to have to desert you for dinner."

"Oh, sweetheart! Why?"

"I simply can't get my paper right for tomorrow," answered Clayton, "I've lost two or three references I can't find in any of my source books here, but they'll be at the museum. You know how important this paper is. And Paddy the watchman will let me in," he added, confidently.

"But you'll starve!"

"I shall have a snack nearby," said Clayton. "Don't worry about me, darling."

"I don't see who else I should worry about," said Rosamund, reasonably. "But if you must go you must. Can I do anything to help?"

"You can pour me out a whisky and soda while I slip into a suit," he answered. "Give me ten minutes, will you?"

"Of course," she said.

They went into the scullery together, then Clayton hurried upstairs, confident that he had passed the situation off smoothly. He wore an old siren or track suit, patched in a dozen places, which had become a habit when working alone in his study. He moved well, and was as lean and fit as a man of fifty could be; virile, too. He had a dressing-room which led into the main bedroom with its huge 'king size' bed; Rosamund's dressing-room opened off on the other side, and each led to a bathroom. He stripped, was under the shower for no more than a minute, towelled vigorously, then put on a lightweight undervest and pants and a dark tweed suit. He went to his study to get the manuscript, which was in truth finished to the last dotted i, and in less than fifteen minutes he turned into the morning-room which was also used by Rosamund for sewing and oddments. She was there. She hadn't changed but the headscarf was gone and her hair fell almost to her shoulders. In some lights, and this was one, she looked little older than on the day she had married him, twenty-three years ago. His whisky and soda and her Martini were already poured, and they lifted their glasses.

"Prosit."

"Happy paper-making," she said lightly.

"Paper-mak— Oh, I see." He laughed. "I'll drink to that!"

"Oliver," she said a moment later.

"Yes?"

"Will this year's conference be as fully attended as ever?"

"More so, I think. Why?"

"I wondered. The interest grows year by year, doesn't it?"

"In the origin of mammals, yes."

"In the origins of man," she countered. "Do you ever wish you travelled as much today as you used to?"

He was startled by the question, and pondered it for a few moments before answering: "I don't think so, darling. I think if I wanted to travel more, I would. Do *you* want to travel more?"

"No," she answered, very quickly and positively. "No, darling. I'm the old Cancerian—I love my home and love to stay in it. I don't think it would worry me if I never went away from London again! But I sometimes wonder, particularly after you went to Australia earlier this year, if you would like to travel more. You found something of great importance there, didn't you?"

"Yes," Professor Clayton said. "Of supreme importance."

After what seemed a long time, Rosamund said without reproach in her voice but with obvious wistfulness: "And you don't feel you can tell me what it was?"

Very quietly, he answered: "No, darling. I can't explain why and I'm sorry if I hurt you by my reticence, but I can confide in no one—no one at all—until I read my paper at the conference. You'll be there. You'll understand why, when you hear what I have to say. It is *not* personal, I swear to you."

"I want to believe that," Rosamund said almost reluctantly. "You will never know how much I want to believe that! There are times when you seem to want to shut me out of part of your life, and—" She broke off, and put her lips to her glass, quickly. "Oh, I'm talking a lot of nonsense and you want to get off. Don't mind me. I know you wouldn't keep this to yourself without a good reason."

"But I do mind," he said. Tonight of all nights, how much he thought of her! In spite of what she had been saying and her rather nostalgic mood she looked relaxed and free from anxiety. Perhaps that was her greatest quality: to be calm and serene and content, never to harass him or make him feel edgy or apprehensive. She was above all things such a complete person, self-sufficient and all-satisfying. "What do you sometimes wonder?"

"Whether you would like to travel more and live alone, but stay at home only because you know I prefer to be here."

"I stay at home because it's where I prefer to be," he answered her.

Something made him look away from her; no doubt, a stab of his own conscience. He moved towards the window, a companion one to his, which overlooked a different part of the walled garden. Here were rosebeds and the flowering shrubs and some dwarf fruit trees; it was a small garden but as nearly perfect as could be, and Rosamund maintained it without help of any kind; from digging and mulching to cutting grass and pruning. In this half-light, a strange one because a huge raincloud was hiding the afterglow except towards the north, the garden had an ethereal look.

"I half expect to see the little people emerge at this time of the evening," he said. "It's quite beautiful, darling."

"I think it's going to be a very good year for roses," Rosamund observed. "And the daffodils—I've never seen anything like them. Can you spare five minutes?"

"Of course."

"Let me top up your glass," said Rosamund.

It was fresh outside, yet warm enough. They linked arms, while he carried his whisky and soda, and she left hers on a garden stool. The grass, damp but not soggy, was springy underfoot. The perfume from the flowering currants and from two flowering cherry trees hidden from each window, was subtle and yet penetrating. There was a hint of the odour of new mown grass. On the side where he had first seen her that evening, the clumps of daffodils were massed, thick as tall grass, with the full trumpets waving. Perhaps because it was getting dark, nothing seemed out of place.

"There isn't even an untidy blade of grass," he remarked.

"You wait until you see it in the light of morning!" she retorted.

Soon, they were back in the house, and a few moments afterwards he was on his way to the garage, where they kept two cars, his a relict of remembered youth, an M.G., hers a new Morris 1800. She did not come to see him off. It was an unwritten law in the household that no one was seen further than the front door.

The engine started at a pull of the self-starter; at first, it roared, but before he was at the end of the street—Beacon Road—it had settled down. The street lamps were on and there were lights at many windows, while other cars had parking lights on, or else their headlamps, dimmed. This road curved several times, and it was five minutes before he was on the main road for Swiss Cottage and the heart of London.

Usually, by now, Rosamund was out of his mind; in her own world, which he shared only when with her. But not tonight. She was everywhere he looked. She was in the windows he passed and in the driving seats of cars which passed him. The transition from one world to another, usually automatic and made without any conscious thought, simply did not take place. As he drew near St. John's Wood and then took the turning through Regent's Park, he was aware only of Ida but only because he made himself think of her. Usually, this was *her* private world; of the open spaces of the park and then the grey houses near the museum itself, a part of London where he seldom brought Rosamund. By the time he reached Mandeville Street, where Ida lived, it was quite dark except for street and car lights. Traffic was light, for this was not a main thoroughfare.

Ida lived at 29, in a top—third—floor flat.

There were spaces for parking nearby and he slipped into one almost opposite the front door of Number 29. The light in Ida's front room window was on but the curtains were drawn. He fastened the canvas cover over the seats of the M.G. and turned towards the house. This street was like many in the Bloomsbury area, all the houses having two steps leading up to the front door, most of the walls grey or once-yellow brick, the doors and windows painted, black predominating, white and pale blue following. Lights glinted and scintillated from old-fashioned London style gas lamps, and reflected on brass knockers, doorknobs and letter-boxes.

This house was his.

The two bottom floors were occupied by a small, exclusive magazine. The upstairs flat, in its way luxurious, was Ida's—in her name and legally hers even though for so many years he had paid all the outgoings.

The front door was locked.

He let himself in with a key, and then pressed the bell-push marked *Mrs. Ida Spray* and closed the front door quietly. A flight of stairs faced him; there was a partition right across the hall which gave the magazine offices comparative seclusion. At the top of the second flight of stairs was a black-painted doorway, marked *Private*; and as he approached this opened and Ida appeared.

It was obvious that she had been crying.

That was the more surprising because Clayton could not remember having seen her cry. Angry, yes; bitter, furious, even hysterical, but never tearful. Almost for the first time in his life he compared her with Rosamund, as if the two women were standing side by side. Ida was a head shorter, broader, thicker-set, and in middle-age she had become heavier. She wasn't fat, and still had a remarkable figure; a little taller and she would have been statuesque. Her features were broad, there was even a hint of the Mongolian about her face, but her skin was without blemish and she was remarkably handsome in a rare fashion.

She put out her hands.

He was two or three steps below her and so could not fail to see her slim ankles and her tiny waist—tiny, in spite of her breadth of shoulder and body. She had small hands, too; and delicate. He took them and she drew him forward onto a half-landing. He pushed the door to with his foot, and they stood very close together. He slid his arm about her waist and tilted her head up by the chin, and then kissed her.

"I'm terribly sorry," he said.

"I know you must be."

"Is there any news?"

"Not a word," she answered.

"Why on earth should Kevin do such a thing?"

Ida did not answer, and with his heightened sensitivity he was keenly aware of that omission. She deliberately did not answer his question, and that could mean that she knew why but didn't want to tell him yet. She twisted round and led the way upstairs.

The flat, he knew, was surprisingly roomy.

There was one large living-room, pleasantly furnished, and a kitchen leading off; then a kind of alcove, off which led one bathroom and bedroom. Up a flight of six shallow steps was a second, larger bedroom and bathroom: Kevin's. As a child's and now as a teenager's it was perfectly equipped.

On a round table in the living-room were bottles and glasses, ready for Oliver. He saw that both the glasses were empty and dry; she was not one to turn to drink for solace. She liked Scotch whisky on ice, in the American style, while he preferred his 'warm' with a dash of soda. She wore a pale brown suit of a smooth textured material; she had natural good taste.

"Have you been able to think of anyone he might have gone to?" he asked as he scooped ice from a bowl.

"I've telephoned several of his friends at the college, and none of them knows where he is—or at least, none of them admits to knowing."

"Girl friends?" he asked.

"Kevin? He has no serious girl friends."

"At his age, that makes him unusual."

"Yes," said Ida, looking at him queerly. "He is an unusual boy, Oliver." She took her drink and sipped; as he drank a third of his at a gulp. It was proving more of a strain than he had expected, and he had no doubt that it was because he had to keep the news of the blackmail to himself. Certainly he had no choice, he could not add to her burden tonight.

"You would know if he had any girl friends," Clayton said.

"Yes, I would."

An idea shot into his head, startling him, one which had never been there before, almost bewildering in its force. He looked at her, startled by himself, but didn't speak. When she had said 'he is an unusual boy, Oliver', could she have meant that Kevin was queer? Homosexual? Could that explain her certainty that he had no girl friends? Surely if that were so, at some time or other she would have told him so, would have wanted advice: or at least, wanted him to approach doctors who could advise. The idea came strongly but he did not want to put it into words.

"Ida," he asked, breaking the ice, "what was the quarrel about?"

She took another sip, but didn't answer. He moved close to her and put a hand on the back of hers. Had he hit on the truth? Was Kevin a homosexual, and had she discovered it only last night, thus provoking a quarrel? It would explain everything, even her rare tears.

"Tell me," he said. "It will do you good to talk."

"I'm not so sure it will," she answered.

Half-seriously, half in raillery, he said in a stronger voice: "Well, if it won't do you good, it will probably be good for me."

She stared intently but did not answer.

At any other time it would have been easier to be patient, understanding, kind, but his own inner tension was so great that it was almost a physical effort not to raise his voice. He had never known Ida like this. She had always been the matter-of-fact, down-to-earth person who called a spade a spade; not uncouth and not unkind, but by nature very forthright. Now she was looking at him from beneath her lashes as if she were being deliberately provocative. He must not let himself show his impatience, the greater her need the greater his effort had to be.

He sat down beside her and slid an arm round her shoulders.

"Ida," he said again, "I am dreadfully sorry. And I did come the moment I knew about what had happened. If there is anything I can do, I will."

"I don't think there is," she said. She did not shrug herself free from his arm but neither did she show any sign of welcoming it, as she would normally. "There might have been a few weeks ago, even a few days ago, but not now. It's too late."

"Oh, come," protested Oliver, tightening his grip and making her turn to face him, "I don't understand you. I wish I did, but I really don't understand what you mean. How could I have helped a few days ago but not now? If there is anything—"

She shrugged herself free, and stood up, beginning to pace the room, looking down at him all the time. When she spoke it was in a low-pitched, bitter voice which carried him back over the years to their early days.

"We quarreled over you," Ida stated. "He's suspected for a long time that you're his father, and took me by surprise when he asked if it were true. Just the expression on my face must have confirmed it. He hates you for refusing to acknowledge him and he hates me because I've never tried to make you. I won't go into the things he called me, even without those it was bad enough. He said he would never come back, never spend a night under my roof again. And although at the time I prayed that he didn't mean it, I feel quite, *quite* sure that he did."

About that time, Roger West was still at his office, finishing all he could find including newspaper reports of the three 'suicides'. One, in fact, might yet be proved to have been accidental death: Norman Akers, one of the up and coming younger men in the British Aeronautics industry, had crashed in an old Gypsy Moth in which he had often flown for fun; no newspaper had suggested that it might have been suicide, but two reports, one from Akers's secretary-and-mistress, and one from his mechanic who had seen him off, each suggested that he had gone off that day in a strangely brittle mood—a savage mood.

The second case was indisputably suicide. Sir Jeremy Godden, a member of a small commercial banking company, had got heavily into debt, 'borrowed' from the bank's account and, apparently knowing he could never hide the facts for long, had thrown himself in front of a tube train. His partners in the firm were making good the losses.

So far, little was known about Sir Douglas Fellowes's reason except what he had said in his suicide note:

28

Nothing even remotely connected with my post in Her Majesty's Civil Service is at stake.

I have reason to believe that I have cancer of the most malignant kind. This is my one and only reason for what I am about to do.

He had gone from his office to his club, and stabbed himself through the neck.

There were other suicides, of course, but none in this short period from the same class of society; and each one had friends and relatives who were probably pushing the Home Secretary to find out the truth.

4

Ugly Truth

Oliver Clayton sat very still as he looked at Ida, after she had told him the simple truth. Years ago the question of acknowledging his parenthood had deeply troubled him, but as time had passed he had come almost to accept the pretended relationship, since anything else would mean that Rosamund would have to know. Why he had not admitted to himself that Kevin would one day become overwhelmingly curious about the relationship he would never know. His 'father' was a shadowy figure; hadn't it been inevitable that he would one day question the truth of his mother's story—that his father had died in an accident? In a way, no doubt, he had realised this but had always pushed it to the back of his mind. Or, more truthfully, persuaded himself that it would never come into the open.

Ida was staring at him; he had no idea what was in her mind.

"Did you tell him?" he asked.

"No. But I admitted it when he—he told me."

"Of course. You had to," he said mechanically. "Do you know how he found out?"

"No."

"Was it—" He went to her and held out his hands, but she didn't take them. "Was it very ugly?"

"Yes," she replied, "it was a hell of an ugly scene, and I felt—" She caught her breath. "Oh, what does it matter?"

Oliver didn't reply, and after a while, Ida went on:

30

"I thought he might have got in touch with you."

"He didn't."

"I bet you're glad he didn't," she said, bitterly. "I bet you're as glad as hell. Your precious home and your precious Rosamund—*they're* safe."

This time, he took her hands firmly, and then sank down onto the seat beside her, making her turn round; and she showed no hesitation in facing him and made no attempt to pull herself free. Her lips were drawn tightly and he could see the lines of pain at her eyes.

At last, he said: "I need a little time to think, Ida, time to try to help to get him back."

"He'll never come back!"

"He might," Oliver Clayton said.

"You know bloody well he'll never come back!" She snatched her hands away, clenching them so tightly he thought she would strike him. "He's been driven away because he found out that his father is ashamed of him because he's a bastard and ashamed of his mother because she's a whore. My *God*, if I had my time over again I'd go up to that precious wife of yours and I'd hold the baby up in front of her and I'd cry: 'Do you want the brat, he's your husband's. Do you want him'?" She sprang to her feet and began to pace the room, hands clenched by her sides, face deathly pale, eyes wild and bright. "If I had my time over again do you know what I'd do to you before I'd let you touch me? I'd castrate you, that's what I'd do! Dear Rosamund, poor Rosamund, chaste Rosamund—well, she didn't give you a son, *I* gave you the only son you've ever had, and what did you do? You turned your back on him, spurned him, were ashamed of him. Isn't that true?" She sprang towards him and shook her tiny, tight-clenched fists under his nose and screeched: "Go on, deny it—deny that you turned your back on him, you never admitted he was your son. *Deny it!*"

He thought she really would strike him, but he did not move even to raise a hand to protect himself. Her lips were drawn back over her teeth, the one gold cap glittered; he could see the tip of her tongue, he could see her breasts rising and falling, her nostrils quivering; he had never seen her in such a rage.

"Go on!" she cried. "Deny it!"

"I can't deny it," he replied at last, and obviously his words so surprised her, although they should not, that she backed away a pace, and lowered her clenched fists.

"I wish I could," he went on.

"Well, you can't. It's too late now."

"Is it?" he asked. "Is it really?"

She frowned, the peak of her anger past. He did not move or do anything to bring back the rage. An expression which might have been of compassion touched her face for a moment; he could not see his own, the degree of his distress.

"What—what do you mean?" she demanded.

"We must find him," Clayton said. "*I* must find him. And then—"

"*Acknowledge* him?"

"I—must." How inevitable it was.

"But now so much time has passed—"

"I must," Clayton repeated, almost roughly. "I wish to God I had, years ago."

She said: "But—*Rosamund*."

He did not need reminding about Rosamund. He did not doubt that it would hurt her unbearably, bring her whole life crashing down on her but the penalty of the long silence was too great. The blackmail—and now Kevin. Either was really enough on its own, together they were too powerful to ignore. Ida was looking at him as if she could not really believe what he was saying, and a kind of wonder appeared in her eyes, but suddenly bitterness flowed back.

"Even if you meant it," she said, "it would be too late."

"We'll get him back," he said.

"You didn't see how he behaved last night, or you wouldn't say that."

32

"Darling," he said. "I know it's useless to say I'm sorry but I am—terribly, terribly sorry about last night, about the years. I shall tell Rosamund. And then I'll help to look for Kevin. He's bound to keep in touch with some of his friends. We'll tell them what I've done, that—that there'll be no more rejection of him, no more of this 'uncle' nonsense, and he'll come back." He spoke with great confidence and in that moment he felt quite sure of himself, although at the back of his mind there was awareness of and apprehension about the inevitable consequences.

It must be soon. Now that the decision was made, he must not leave it long.

"Oliver," she said, chokily.

"Yes, darling?"

"Are you sure Rosamund will want a divorce?"

"Yes," he said.

"After—so many years, it seems so bloody awful."

"Don't try to dissuade me," he said. "I've been long enough coming to the decision, for God's sake don't try to discourage me now."

"Would you—"

"I shall tell her."

"Would you like to sleep on it?" she insisted, almost timidly.

"I shall tell her tonight."

"Oliver," she said, a soft and different creature from the termagant she had been a few moments before, "you don't have to, for me."

"I have to, at long last, for me—"

"That's the only reason why you should," she said, heavily. "Not for me and not to try to win Kevin's affection."

He was startled. "Not for Kevin?"

"If you did, if you broke up your home for Kevin, you might learn to hate him. And what good would it do if you hated each other?" She almost laughed. "Darling, it's not like you to be impetuous. You mustn't be, now. You must give yourself time to think about it." When he didn't answer, just raised and dropped his hands, she went on: "I'm sorry I behaved like that just now."

"Don't be silly," he said. "I am unscathed!"

"You nearly weren't."

"I know," he said, wryly.

They stared at each other for what seemed a long time, and then both laughed; not deeply and not for long, but enough to draw the rest of the tension out of them. He slid his arm about her waist and they kissed lightly, then went into the kitchen where she put the kettle on for tea. He leaned against the draining-board, watching her as she busied herself and the kettle began to sing. Suddenly, she asked:

"Where will you have dinner?"

"I'd thought, at the club."

"Where are you supposed to be?"

"In the museum, admitted by the night watchman at the side door!"

They laughed again, and then Ida asked: "Would you like a steak, cully? I've one in the freezer. Or some bacon and eggs? Or—"

He stopped her, by saying: "Will you mind being alone for an hour or two?"

"No," she said. "No, not now."

"Then I will go to the club," he said. "I need—" He hesitated.

"A rehearsal?"

"In a way, yes."

"Oliver," she said, picking up the laden tea tray, "I would rather you slept on it. I know it must have been awful when I lost my cool like that, but I'm over the top now. I shall be all right. And Kevin might come back and—and even see reason, especially if you talk to him. I don't think you should do anything with Rosamund on impulse, I really don't."

When they were back in the living-room he realised that he was at another crossroads. She believed his one reason for deciding to face Rosamund was Kevin, and he wanted to believe that the boy would have been enough, but was not sure. Kevin and the blackmail together—and now, Ida had to be told about the blackmail, or, when she found out, she would know that he had at least half-lied to her. He waited for her to pour out tea, which was very strong, before he began to tell her. In the telling, he wondered whether she would turn on him again; whether she would think he had been planning to tell Rosamund even before he had arrived here, and he feared what her reaction would be if she came to that conclusion.

He read alarm in her eyes; and then, concern; and before he had finished she had put her tea on the table and was on her knees in front of him, clasping his hands.

"Oh my darling," she said. "My poor darling. You had that to contend with even before I telephoned you. Oh, Oliver, I couldn't be more sorry, I really couldn't, but—*this* needn't make you tell Rosamund, either."

He was puzzled by her train of thought but had no doubt it was clear and direct to her; as everything was clear and direct.

"I don't understand," he said.

"Darling, you must go to the police," said Ida, as if there was no possible doubt. "They'll help and they'll find the blackmailer, but they'll keep it secret. They never disclose the victim's name in a blackmail case. And—and if I could find Kevin and tell him this he might feel very differently—he'll know how awful it must be for you.

"Don't tell Rosamund anything yet, darling," Ida pleaded. "Go and see the police."

Now that she had talked of the police, there was no other possible course; it was obviously the thing to do. The only thing to do.

Roger West put down the telephone, after talking to Janet his wife and telling her he would be home in about half-an-hour. Their son Richard and his girl-friend Lindy were at home, so Janet was not lonely; she was probably telling the youngsters some of the highlights of their trips through the big game parks, and showing some of the coloured transparencies on a small hand-viewer. It was ironic that he should have had so little to do all day and yet not be able to spend the evening at home; before they had gone away, Janet had hated the lonely evenings so much that there had been periods of acute emotional tension between them.

A shadowy thought hovered: that if he were under too much working pressure, the tension might come back. He pushed the idea aside; the holiday had done Janet at least as much good as it had done him.

He pulled the papers about the three suspected suicides towards him.

Coppell had no doubt sent for him late in the day because of Fellowes's suicide. Could there be any significance in the way that he had used of dispatching onself? So far Roger had no idea whether the fear of cancer had been justified; he did not even know whether Fellowes had been seriously ill and under a doctor. He would have to make up his mind when to visit and question the family. In fact he had to make up his mind about a great number of things: and he mustn't take too long.

First: were these 'suicides'—unless Aker had died in an accident?

Second: if all three were suicides as two inquests had decided, could there be any common motivation? At first sight, no: a civil servant of great distinction, a man equally distinguished in aeronautics, a third involved in commercial banking. Clearly, money could be a common factor; so could blackmail; but he was a long, long way from having any reason to think there was a connection between the deaths.

His telephone bell rang.

It surprised him, because few knew that he was working late, and fewer—hardly any—knew that he was involved in this inquiry. It might be someone who simply wanted to welcome him back.

"Superintendent West," he said into the telephone.

36

"I wasn't sure whether you were still there," a man replied. The familiar voice was that of Chief Inspector Miller, of *Information*. "I've had a call from a V.I.P., sir, who says he wants to talk in confidence to a senior officer here, and there are no senior officers free. I wondered if you would have a word with him."

"Where is he?" asked Roger. "On the telephone?"

"No, sir," replied Miller. "He simply said he was on his way, and would be here in about twenty minutes. He's Professor Oliver Clayton, the anthropologist. I asked him if it couldn't wait until the morning but he said he has to be at a conference of anthropologists—the one they hold annually, sir—from ten o'clock onwards, and this business won't wait."

Not dreaming that there could be a connection between this and the files on his desk, Roger said readily enough: "I'll see him. Ask the receptionist to advise me when he's arrived, will you, and then bring him right up."

"I'll do that, sir!" Miller sounded grateful.

Roger rang off, looked through the files again, and was uneasily aware that a lot of time had passed since the deaths of Aker and Gooden, and only by talking to their business associates, friends and families could he hope to learn more than there was in these scanty reports. He was so absorbed in what he was doing that the telephone bell startled him when it rang; twenty minutes had positively raced away.

"This is reception, sir. A Professor Oliver Clayton—"

"Send him up," Roger repeated. "I'll meet him at the lift." He rang off on the man's 'thank you' and got up immediately, walking out of the still unfamiliar office to the still unfamiliar passages of the fourth floor of the new building which housed Scotland Yard. He was at the lifts a minute or two before one opened, and a taller, lantern-jawed, impressively distinguished man stepped out.

Roger had no doubt at all, after a glance at his expression, that this man was in grave trouble.

5

West Listens

"The first thing I must ask," said Oliver Clayton, even before he sat down by the side of Roger's desk, "is that for the time being at least this matter be treated in strict confidence."

"If it's possible, it will be," Roger replied.

"It *must* be!" Clayton insisted, tensely.

What he had to do, reflected Roger, was to ease the man's tension. The glitter in the eyes, grip of hands, even the posture of the body all betrayed the fact that his visitor's nerves were at screaming point. He pushed an armchair so that it was easy for the other to drop into it, and sat in the swivel chair at his desk, which was set cornerwise so that he had the light from the window by day, and always faced the door. The office was reasonably spacious; sparsely furnished with modern furniture.

"You know, sir," he said with a smile, "if you were to tell me you'd just committed murder, I couldn't treat it in confidence."

"Oh, don't be absurd!" Clayton barked.

"If it's something which I can keep in confidence, I will," Roger promised.

"I don't mean you," said Clayton. "Not personally. I mean the police force."

"Try us, sir."

"I am being blackmailed!" Clayton blurted out.

Yes, thought Roger; blackmail had been a safe bet from the moment he had set eyes on this man. Professor Oliver Clayton, aged fifty-five, Fellow of the Royal Society, one of the three most famous anthropologists in the country, the six most famous in the world, known colloquially as one of the 'Old Fossils'. The essentials he had found in *Who's Who in Science* and *Who's Who* since Miller had given him the caller's name, the 'Old Fossil' stuck from some newspaper recollection. What had such a man done, in the past, to be blackmailed? The idle question was absurd.

"If you are being blackmailed," Roger said, "be absolutely sure we shall conduct all inquiries in strict confidence and even if it came to a trial your name would not be mentioned unless quite exceptional circumstances demanded it."

Clayton said, in a husky voice: "Thank you. Thank you indeed."

"When did the blackmailing begin?" asked Roger.

"This—this afternoon."

"So recently?" Roger warmed to this man. "It isn't often we get notice so quickly. Did someone come to see you?" He would have to draw the story out, in the beginning, but before long it would probably become a flood, unprompted.

"No. A man telephoned."

"And demanded money for his silence?"

"Yes," Clayton said, leaning back in his chair. "He demanded twenty thousand pounds. I had no idea at all that anyone knew—knew my secret, but since the man made his demand I've realised that dozens probably know it. I—I have a son. I—"

The flood began slowly, and ran off from time to time in a dozen different streams, some floods in themselves. Roger listened intently but made no notes and asked no questions; one or the other could distract a man in Clayton's mood and make the flood dry up. Later, he could ask whatever he needed and get the story in full perspective and in proper order. In fact he was able to do that as the other talked. The twenty-year-old liaison, the illegitimate son, the patient 'other woman' and the sudden, devastating realisation that someone else knew and was prepared to tell his wife.

Clayton thought it was a unique story, but he, Roger, had heard a dozen, perhaps twenty or thirty similar in outline, different only in detail. But still he said nothing.

"I went to see Ida this evening," Clayton said, "because her—" He broke off, moistened his lips and then correct: "Because our son had run away from her. It transpired that he had realised I was his father . . ."

This part of the story was touching and sad, but still not unique; all the frailities of human beings passed across the desks of the officers at Scotland Yard sooner or later; all the varieties and the vagaries of human behaviour, too. But it was easier to understand what had driven Clayton here so soon; Roger breathed a silent blessing on the head of the woman Ida, who had driven him to come here tonight.

At last, Clayton stopped, and drew out a handkerchief to wipe his forehead. Roger opened a cupboard on the far side of his desk as he asked:

"Is that everything, Professor?"

"Apart possibly from details, yes. And—" He broke off.

"And what, sir?"

"Well—it is hardly relevant in some ways but extremely important in others. I have to make a speech which I regard as of exceptional significance to the International Anthropological Conference. The 'Old Fossils' themselves. I need to spend all my energies on checking and preparing the presentation of that. It was terribly tempting to buy time, Superintendent."

"You will be much easier in your mind now, sir, and able to concentrate." Roger wondered fleetingly what could seem of such importance to the anthropologist in this man, but that was not likely to be a fruitful line of inquiry. He took out a bottle of whisky, two bottles of soda water and two glasses. "I am extremely glad you've come to us so quickly. We can do two things at once. Keep an eye open for Kevin, without making it official, of course—Miss Spray will be easier in her mind when she knows where he is, won't she?"

"Very much easier," said Clayton, gratefully. "She has been known for many years as Mrs. Spray."

"I'll enter her as Mrs. Spray on the records," Roger promised. "Will you have a whisky and soda?"

Clayton looked at the bottle almost longingly, but shook his head.

"I really shouldn't," he said. "I had no dinner and it would go straight to my head. Superintendent, what do you think are the chances of finding this man?"

"In the circumstances, good," Roger replied promptly.

"Do you think I should get the money and—" Clayton broke off, and raised his hands to his forehead. "Really, I hardly know what I'm doing or saying or thinking," he went on in a hopeless-sounding tone. "One moment I am quite sure that I must tell all of this to my wife—and if I do, then the fellow will have no grounds for blackmail. The next, I'm desperately afraid of her finding out." He drew his hands from his forehead, and as he looked at Roger, his eyes seemed to burn. Almost as an incantation, he went on: "What am I to do? What *am* I to do?"

It was an appeal from one human being to another; not from a blackmail victim to a police officer. And Roger both sensed and responded to the appeal. He put the whisky aside, and said quite briskly:

"First, you're going to have a meal, sir. Would you care to come up to our canteen with me? We could talk as we eat—"

"Haven't *you* eaten?"

"Not since lunch," Roger answered. "We can have a table where we won't be overheard." He was anxious for Clayton to accept this invitation; over a meal they could become much better acquainted, formality would be almost gone, and this man would probably tell him many things which, at present, were hidden in the corners of his mind. He could clarify his own thoughts, too. If he were to catch this blackmailer then it would have to be redhanded; either while he was demanding money or accepting it. What chance was there of either if Clayton did immediately tell his wife the truth?

Probably, thought Roger, he would be prepared to let the blackmailer think he still had his stranglehold.

"I would very much like to join you," Clayton said, at last. "You are very kind and understanding, Superintendent."

"I've lived long enough to know that few people can think clearly on an empty stomach, still less make decisions," Roger replied. "Shall we go?"

Much of the big, L-shaped canteen was closed off; and only a few of the tables in the open section were occupied. The cafeteria line was empty, there was some roast beef and Yorkshire pudding with baked potatoes and cabbage which looked as appetising as if it were on the kitchen table of a good home cook.

"We'll come back for sweet," Roger said. "What would you like to drink with your meal?"

"Is there beer?"

"Of course," Roger said.

"Then a light ale, please."

They sat down well away from anyone else, and it was an unwritten law that if a senior officer was at a table with a guest, then that table was given a wide berth; for how else would he want to talk but confidentially. It was Clayton who did most of the talking, filling out the picture of his home life, his fear of divorce, his fear of being ostracised by his daughters; and the newer fear, that Kevin might do something desperate in his present mood.

"I really shouldn't worry about that," Roger said. "Very few actually ever reach the point of feeling that life isn't worth living. He isn't on drugs, is he?"

"I think you can be sure he's not."

"Girl friends?" asked Roger.

"I had a feeling—it's no more—that he might be homosexual," Clayton replied. "It was something his mother said, but—don't say I told you, whatever you do!"

"This is all very much in confidence," Roger reminded him. "What would you like to follow, sir?"

"I *think* I saw a baked jam roll which looked most tempting," Clayton said.

"Two jam rolls and some coffee?" Roger said with a laugh. "I'll get it."

He went off, leaving the other man alone at the table to ponder over what he had said and thought. He liked the man West enormously. There was nothing remotely official or red tape about him, he was one of the most natural of men, and Clayton was amazed that he had talked to anyone so freely. He felt quite safe with West; confident that any advice the man gave would be worth following—or at the very least, worth the closest possible attention. He watched him coming back with a laden tray, two cups of steaming coffee, two large portions of the jam roll, baked crisply and with strawberry jam oozing out.

Soon, they were eating.

Soon, West was saying: "You're most acute immediate problem is whether to tell your wife, isn't it?"

"It is indeed," Clayton said, ruefully. "I still vacillate dreadfully. Ida wanted me to sleep on it, but—" He broke off, and paused with a piece of the jam roll on the end of his fork. "I'm not sure she's right. I am really not sure. Superintendent—"

"Yes?"

"Supposing I don't tell Rosamund. Supposing you catch the blackmailer and he goes on trial. How far does this confidence go? My name would be suppressed of course, but a great many officials here and presumably at court would know. Would it really be practicable to conceal the truth from my wife and family?"

Roger answered without the slightest hesitation.

"It would be extremely difficult unless she were out of London—or preferably out of England—for the period of the trial. She would never be told officially but you yourself would be under very great strain, and the newspapers would make a lot of play with Mr. X. And—" He broke off.

"Please go on," Clayton urged.

"It isn't really my place to," Roger West replied. "In fact I'm not sure that anyone but an old and close friend should say this to you."

He had finished eating, and his grey eyes were very steady as he looked at Clayton. The big room seemed empty except for the two of them, Clayton thought; and he had another, stranger thought: that he had no old and close friend with whom he could discuss this. He hesitated for a long time, and then with a ghost of a smile in his eyes, he said:

"I promise to keep whatever you say in strict confidence. Please tell me what is in your mind."

Roger actually found himself chuckling.

"Then I will," he said, and went on so quickly and with such assurance that it was obvious that he had thought deeply about what he was saying: it was almost as if he had some personal experience on which to draw, he spoke with such feeling. "If you tell your wife now she will know that you need her help and her loyalty, and I would think with such a woman as you have described, you are likely to bring out the best in her. But if you wait until a trial, if you show that you can handle this situation by yourself, and don't need her, then—then I would think she will be deeply hurt, perhaps feeling that you've never needed her. In a way that is far worse than not having deeply loved."

"Nothing could be further from the truth," Clayton asserted, emphatically. "I shall go straight home and tell her." He pushed his chair back and stood up, so eager not to delay that some of those present must have thought he was leaving in anger.

"I'm sure you're wise," Roger said, quietly. "Can I send you home in a police car? Or I could drive you myself. I—"

"I've my car only fifty yards away," Clayton told him. "I'll be happy to go on my own. May I tell you how things turn out?"

"Here's my home telephone number," Roger said, handing him a card.

He saw Oliver Clayton down to street level and into Broadway, where his own car was parked, but did not wait long enough to watch him get into his M.G. and drive off. Had he waited, he might also have seen the man on a motor-cycle who moved away from a spot nearby just after Clayton. But the M.G. went in one direction, cutting through towards Hyde Park, while the motor-cycle roared into Victoria Street and then towards Parliament Square and the floodlit front of Westminster Abbey and the moon-face of Big Ben.

It did not occur to him for a moment that any immediate danger threatened Clayton, and his main preoccupation was how to resolve the situation if the man did tell his wife. Would she—would Clayton, for that matter—go through a charade of pretending with the blackmailer, so as to give the police a chance to catch him?

Still less did it occur to him that there was the remotest connection between the attempt to blackmail Clayton, and the three suicides.

Oliver Clayton, meanwhile, drove towards Hampstead in a very different mood from when he had left. He had no doubt at all that he must tell Rosamund tonight, and there was a curious excitement at the prospect. He was eager to tell her, to face the worst; and Superintendent West had contrived to make him believe that the worst would be nothing like as bad as he had expected. He exerted himself to drive carefully; in such a mood, it would be easy to be reckless. He drove across the poorly-lit heath to Beacon Road, and slowed down as he neared his house in Beacon Drive. He would leave the car in the driveway rather than garage it tonight; it would save a lot of opening and closing of doors. He drove to within a few inches of the double doors of the garage, put the gear into neutral, and turned off the engine.

As he opened the door and climbed out, he saw the shadowy

figures of two men, who rushed at him. He saw their upraised arms and the weapons in them and felt a flood of terror as the first blow fell, with awful pain, across the back of his head.

He heard one phrase: "We'll teach you to go to the police."

Then they rained blows on him and he sank down by the side of the car, making no sound, no longer aware of pain.

Five minutes later, two motor-cyclists, wearing crash helmets and goggles, roared away from Clayton's house. No one took any notice of them, although many heard the sound of the engines—including Rosamund Clayton, so nearby.

6

Near Unto Death

"Good morning, sir."
" 'Morning."
" 'Morning, Handsome!"
" 'Morning, Bill."
"Good morning, good morning, good morning." Roger did not know why he was so conscious of the greetings, in a variety of tones and even greater variety of accents. Scottish and York-shire, Somerset and Welsh, and always the inevitable Cockney, all sounded as he walked along the passages to his office.

It was good to be back.

It was much better this morning than yesterday, because there was plenty waiting to be done. What a strange day yesterday had been. This morning he could expect a demand from Coppell, wanting up-to-the-minute information: he had to decide whether to recommend going back to the friends and families of the first two suicides. There should be a report from the pathologist on Sir Douglas Fellowes; if cancer were confirmed then any ulterior motive could surely be discounted. The Clayton case seemed to him far more promising. He had half-expected a call from Clayton at his home last night; had the Professor's courage failed him at the last moment? If so, would he be at the office early? He was due at his first conference session at the British Musueum so if he were coming here he certainly wouldn't be late.

The two newspapers he had at home had Fellowes's suicide on the front page. Someone, probably Venables the sergeant who worked in the office next to him and was a kind of general factotum, had placed every London morning newspaper on his desk, neatly folded so that the main headlines showed. Three concerned Fellowes and the delicate Common Market negotiations for which he had been partly responsible. The *Daily Globe* came out most strongly with questions at which the other papers only hinted.

Political Cause for Common Market
Expert's 'Suicide'?

Sir Douglas Fellowes, K.C.B.E., one of Britain's most astute and respected Civil Servants, an expert on European Common Market affairs, is believed to have left a suicide note after allegedly stabbing himself to death in a West End club yesterday. The note stated that Sir Douglas believed he had incurable cancer.

The Globe mourns the loss of a great servant of the State.

At the same time, *The Globe* wonders whether all the truth is known. Sir Douglas was believed at one time to be a strong opponent of Great Britain's entry into the Market. The politicians of all parties ignored his advice and opted to join whatever sacrifice it entails.

Was Sir Douglas's illness in any way due to fear and anxiety about the consequences of this political decision? Or his own change of heart? Is it even possible that Sir Douglas had made discoveries about Britain's membership which led to his death?

Roger finished reading, sat back and whistled faintly under his breath. That was strong meat, even for the *Globe*, ever a bitter opponent of Britian's entry into the European Common Market. Between the lines, plain for all to see, was the implication that the death had not in fact been suicide. Even had

48

Coppell not been active about the suicide already, this would have forced him to make an exhaustive inquiry. Directly he had read the article, of course, he would send for him, Roger.

Both of them would have vivid memories of the *Globe* newspaper. Not many months ago it had been taken over by an extreme right wing politicial faction and its policy, at the time, had been close to reasonable. Since then it had been acquired by a small, independent newspaper group, not so right wing as the previous owners but nevertheless reactionary in most political policies. It was strange to find it taking such a strong line now; it was almost as if there had been no change of ownership.

Nonsense! He knew there had been; and the *Globe* wasn't alone in distrusting the Common Market, in wanting Britain to withdraw in splendid isolation.

He scanned the other headlines.

Clearly, Fleet Street was deeply troubled by the death of Sir Douglas Fellowes. As clearly, all of the newspapers wondered if there were any connection between his death and his Common Market activities. Roger opened a folder on his desk, containing letters in this morning and reports on the three suicides which he had studied last night. There was nothing about the autopsy. He called his sergeant on the inter-office instrument and the man answered as quickly as if he had been sitting waiting for the call.

"Venables here, sir."

"Good morning. Is there any word about the pathologist's report on the cause of the death of Sir Douglas Fellowes?"

"Nothing at all, sir." Venables was positive.

"Telephone Dr. Caller's office and ask if the report is ready—we'll fetch it if necessary."

"Sir," said Venables.

"Yes?"

"I telephoned the office twenty minutes ago."

"Well?"

"No one will be in until ten o'clock, sir—Dr. Caller was working late, and so was his chief assistant."

"Call them again at two minutes past ten," ordered Roger, and rang off on the other's 'Very good, sir.' He put the receiver down and caught one of the newspapers in the broad leather strap of his wristwatch, so that the whole pile slid towards the edge of the desk. He grabbed, to save them. The newspapers fanned out, rather like a hand of playing cards, and he caught sight of a few lines in red print beneath the *Stop Press* notice.

He went very still.

It was one of the unbelievable things; so unbelievable that although he read and understood the words he wasn't at first convinced by them. That was only momentary: he read again and the words struck at him as savagely as a physical blow.

Anthropologist Attacked

Professor Oliver Clayton, British representative at today's British Museum Conference of Anthropologists from all over the world, was brutally attacked in the grounds of his Hampstead home last night. Clayton rushed to Hampstead Cottage Hospital. Divisional Police seeking two motor-cyclists.

A.P. News.

He breathed: "My God!" and snatched up the telephone, saying as the Yard operator answered: "Get me Hampstead Cottage Hospital." He rang off, and then scanned the other newspapers but there was nothing more about the attack on Clayton. The telephone bell rang.

"Here's your call to Hampstead Hospital, sir."

"Thanks. And—you still there? . . . Get me Hampstead Division, whoever is in charge, and hold them until I'm through with this call."

"Very good, sir . . . You're through."

It took Roger three minutes to get through to the Secretary, whom it appeared was the only official who could give him any news about Clayton. A brisk-voiced man, the Secretary said:

"Professor Clayton had emergency brain surgery during the night, Superintendent. He is in the intensive care ward, and on the danger list. His wife is at the hospital, one of his daughters is also here." Without a pause the man went on: "The superintendent on night duty at your Divisional Headquarters has been fully informed."

"Yes. Thanks," Roger said. "Has anybody else inquired about the Professor?"

"Several newspapermen, naturally."

"Anyone else?" insisted Roger.

"Not to my knowledge," replied the other man, and for the first time sounded more human being than automaton. "Would you expect someone?"

Roger said quietly: "In confidence—yes."

"Who?" asked the Secretary.

"A close friend of the Professor might call. Can you arrange for her to be given the latest information in strict confidence?"

"I will give instructions that if any close friend telephones the call shall be put through to me at once."

"You're very helpful," Roger said appreciatively. "Thank you—I expect to be in touch soon." He rang off, and sat back for a few moments, wondering whether that had been wise, assuring himself that the hospital secretary would certainly be discreet. Confidential, he thought, and seemed to hear Clayton's voice and to see his troubled face as he had sat in this very office. "My God!" Roger muttered aloud. "He probably went straight home from here and ran into this." On the word 'this' the telephone bell rang again and he picked up the receiver.

"Chief Inspector Lovell of Hampstead Division is on the line, sir."

"Put him through," said Roger, and a moment later: "Jack Lovell?"

"Good morning, sir."

"What's known about the attack on Professor Clayton?" demanded Roger.

"We're gradually getting the picture," Lovell answered confidently. He was a man fifteen years junior to Roger, likely to have a long and successful career at the Yard. "Two motor-cyclists arrived at the back of the house ten minutes before the other. They were seen by a man walking his dog, and who is vague on time but is sure about the sequence of arrivals. The garage is at the side of the house, screened from the road—Pool Road—by bushes and trees. The Professor arrived in his M.G. and turned into the garage driveway. Judging from the blood which splashed the car and congealed on the drive, he was attacked as he got out of the car. Two motor-cycles were seen later at Hampstead Pond by one of our chaps. According to estimates of timing, this must have been about ten minutes or so after the attack. The couple split up at the Pond. One went down towards Swiss Cottage, the other down past Spaniards Inn."

"Descriptions?"

"Both wore crash helmets and goggles," Lovell answered, "but both were small men, each rode a Hokki, each wore a black jacket of leather or plastic, and each wore jeans. I was going to ask for a general call to go out on both."

"Call *Information* and say I authorised it," Roger said. "Aren't Hokkis those powerful Japanese machines fairly new to England?"

"Well—they've only just started to arrive in a big way. Thanks for giving me the go-ahead."

"Anything else?" asked Roger, and went on before the other could reply: "When was Professor Clayton found?"

"Just after midnight, sir, by Mrs. Clayton." Roger found his teeth clenching. "She was worried because he was so late, checked with some authorities at the British Museum where he was supposed to have been and learned that he'd never been there, and went down to the garage—more to look for him than anything else."

"How is she taking things?"

"I haven't seen her myself but Taffy Davies says she was rational and calm after she'd called her doctor and us. Her doctor was out, and a police surgeon with an ambulance reached her first, sir. There was an emergency operation, and she's still at the hospital."

"Thanks," Roger said.

"What's your special interest, sir?" asked Lovell.

"Keep this right under your hat," ordered Roger. "He came to the Yard because he was being blackmailed. He'd been ordered by the blackmailer not to consult the police."

Lovell exclaimed: "Good God! You think he was attacked because he'd been seen to come here?"

"It's obviously possible," Roger replied. "Keep me in close touch. When will Superintendent Cash be in?"

"He's on sick leave, sir. I'm in charge today."

"Then keep me in touch personally," Roger ordered and rang off.

He did not move immediately, but sat motionless. Thoughts flashed through his mind with undisciplined speed, he had to get them in order, had to sort out the significant from the trivia, had to make up his mind what next to do. He was perhaps five minutes, sitting there, before he lifted the inter-office telephone and dialled *Information*. He wished Miller were still on duty but he would have gone an hour—two hours—ago.

"*Information*—Detective Inspector Hamilton," a man said in a faintly Scottish accent.

"Superintendent West here," Roger said. "I want you to get a good description of a youth aged about nineteen or twenty, named Kevin Spray—S-P-R-A-Y—who lives at 29 Mandeville Street, Bloomsbury. When you have it I want the description and a photograph if practical sent to all London and nearby divisions. If the Press make inquiries refer them to me. All clear?"

"Perfectly, sir. Shall I report back to you?"

"Yes," Roger replied. "And Inspector—I want to know whether he runs a motor-cycle, and whether he is big or small."

"Right, sir."

Roger rang off.

He would not have said this to anyone yet, but if Clayton had given him a true picture of his son's mood the previous night then Kevin Spray might have attacked him, out of the frustrated anger and shame of years; might also have been the blackmailer. Had only one motor-cyclist been observed that possibility would have seemed more apparent. Until he knew for certain where the youth had been last night it would be impossible to cross him off the list of suspects for either crime.

But the other possibility, the one which Lovell had voiced, was much the more likely: a cold-blooded attack by blackmailers who wanted money, and hoped to frighten Clayton from going to the police.

Was that more likely?

Wasn't it in fact far-fetched?

If Kevin had wanted to punish him, wouldn't the rational thing have been simply to tell his wife, using talk of twenty thousand pounds as a blind? Once again the fact of two motor-cyclists hampered this line of thought.

He felt the uneasiness which so often preceded a big case; a sense, or premonition, that he was in deeper waters than he knew. And in such a mood, he wanted—he needed—action. Whom should he go to see?

He knew already who it would be: Ida Spray, mother of Kevin and mistress of Clayton. He was on his feet, about to open the communicating door to the sergeant's office and to tell Venables he was going out, when he thought: Coppell! He swung round, picked up the inter-office telephone and dialled the Commander.

Usually his secretary would answer, but this morning it was Coppell himself.

"Commander, C.I.D."

"West here, sir," Roger said. "I have to go out for an hour or two—do you want to see me before I go?"

"I've to go and see the Assistant Commissioner about that piece in the *Globe*," Coppell answered in a growl; obviously he assumed that Roger had seen the article. "Don't be back later than noon." His voice faded as if he were about to put the receiver down, then grew louder again: "Handsome!"

"I'm still here," Roger said.

"Where you're going has to do with the suicides, I take it. I want you to concentrate on those."

"I'll be more sure when I get back," Roger answered, and rang off before Coppell could reply. Two minutes later he was on his way down the street.

7

Mandeville Street

Roger, driving and alone, turned his black Rover 3½ litre into Mandeville Street, and drove along slowly. The terraced houses, in their new paint, had an attraction for him different from any other part of London. They looked solid, yet were pleasing to the eyes. They were joined together, though each was distinctive; the two steps leading to each painted front door were the same, but years of usage had worn them all differently.

Cars were parked at meters on either side of the street.

He espied a vacant place and took it, driving with the unthinking expertise of long practice. He was a dozen houses away from Number 29—not bad at all. He walked briskly towards the house, seeing the board fastened to the wall with an announcement in gilt lettering on black paint. *Excelsior: The Magazine which always rises higher.* Cheap or clever? he wondered, and stepped on freshly whitened steps into a small entrance hall. Immediately opposite the front door was another sign, saying: *First and Second Floor—Editorial. Third Floor—Mrs. Ida Spray.* He went upstairs and found the closed door to the top floor apartment and rang the bell, the push of which was on the right.

So far, he had seen no one.

He heard nothing.

He rang again, as a young man came out of another door,

marked: *Deputy Editor*. He caught a glimpse of a long-haired, long-bearded young man, who took a few steps forward and then turned—virtually pirouetted—on his right heel and went back whence he had come.

The door in front of Roger opened and a woman stood there.

She was short; hardly reaching to his chin. She had pleasant features, and yet was obviously suffering from strain at that moment. He could not fail to notice her full but tightly confined bosom, or her tiny hands and wrists, for these were raised in front of her as if to fend someone off; or, he reminded himself, in welcome for someone she expected.

She had no welcome for him.

"Oh!" she exclaimed, and it was almost a gasp. "I thought it was—" She faltered, and then went on weakly: "Someone else."

"Did you think it was your son?" asked Roger.

She drew in a deep breath, and there was alarm, perhaps fear, in her golden brown eyes. She did not speak for a moment, but then managed to ask:

"Who—who are you?"

"The police officer whom Professor Clayton came to see last night," Roger answered.

She said in a funny little voice: "So he did come. And—you know about me." She closed her eyes, but only momentarily, stood aside for him to pass, and let him lead the way up the worn wooden steps, slippery with polish. He waited on the tiny landing and she led him into a room which overlooked narrow, walled gardens, all well-kept, and the backs of houses opposite.

"My name is West," Roger told her. "Superintendent West."

She still had her hands in front of her bosom; now he was sure that what she was doing was fending off something which she did not want to face. The anguish in her eyes reminded him vividly of Clayton last night, and she was breathing heavily.

Suddenly, words burst out of her: "Do you know how Oliver is?"

"Yes," Roger answered, gently. "Very gravely ill, but with a chance."

"Oh God," she gasped. "Oh God. He—he's not dead, then?"

"I telephoned the hospital only half-an-hour ago."

"Oh God," she repeated. "I—I daren't."

"If you telephone and ask for the Secretary, telling him I told you to call, he'll speak to you at any time and give you an up-to-the-minute report," Roger assured her.

"You—you arranged that?"

"You were bound to be greatly distressed."

"Distressed," she echoed. "Oh, dear God." She backed to a high-seated chair and dropped into it, tiny feet dangling inches off the ground. There was new intensity in her gaze and he had little doubt of the cause. "Did he—did he tell you that my son was—had run away?"

"Yes."

"Have you found Kevin? I mean—"

"I know who Kevin is," Roger interrupted. "But I'm afraid he's not been found; we've only just started to look for him. Mrs. Spray, do you think his emotions would be so intense that he might seek revenge on his father?"

"I can't believe he would," muttered Ida Spray. "I simply can't believe he would attempt to kill or blackmail his father."

Roger spoke next with soft-voiced deliberation. In one way his question was cruel; in another it was kind, making her talk about her inmost fears, and making her face the worst.

"You haven't answered my question. Do you think he was so emotionally distressed that he might seek revenge?"

"He wouldn't do it!" she cried.

"He was in a furious rage, wasn't he?"

"Yes, but—but he's not violent. He hates violence!"

"Angry, bitter and terribly hurt," Roger insisted.

"Oh, God," she repeated. "Yes."

"Mrs. Spray," Roger said, "has your son a motor-cycle?"

She didn't answer, but her silence was answer enough. He

58

waited for a few moments, and then went on in the quiet but persistent voice he had used throughout this interview:

"Is it a Hokki?"

She bowed her head, and whispered: "Yes."

"Where does he keep it?"

"In—in a garage in Kent Street."

"Did he go off on it, yesterday?"

"I don't know."

"Is he a member of a motor-cycling club or group?"

She whispered: "Yes."

"Can you tell me the names of some of them—preferably starting with the leader," he asked.

"It's—it's a University club," she said. "He's studying political economy, and gets involved in—in demonstrations. Kevin is—is the leader. I—" She was speaking slowly, with long pauses between each word, and her breathing came with difficulty. "I only know one—one of the others. His name is Freddie Higginbottom. He came here to a meal once, and I know he and Kevin are—are close friends."

She knew from that *Stop Press*, of course, that the police were looking for two motor-cyclists; and there was no doubt at all what she feared; what, in fact, she believed. That in his rage her son and his friend had waylaid Clayton, and attacked and nearly killed him. She could say it was impossible, that her son would not do such a thing, hating violence: but it was her dread that he had.

Roger asked: "How long has your son known who his father was?"

"I—I don't know."

"Didn't he tell you before last night?"

"No," she said, helplessly. "No, I'd no idea he knew."

"Could he have known before?"

"I suppose so. What difference does it make?"

"A great deal," Roger assured her, feeling the need to help and ease this woman's fear, yet at the same time he did not want to give her false hope; nor let her think that his sympathies were too much with her. "If he's known for some time he would hardly rush off in a fit of rage last night, would he? If he committed the crime you fear he did, it would surely be out of shock as well as anger. Isn't that reasonable?"

A gleam of what might have been hope shone in her eyes.

"Yes, I suppose—I suppose it would. But I don't know whether he'd known for some time. He was so angry last night I thought he must have found out just before. I—I went to Australia earlier this year, with—when Professor Clayton was there. I noticed a change in Kevin soon after I got back. He found out we were in Australia together, and I suppose it set him thinking. But I don't know for certain—I simply don't know."

"Do you know where Freddie Higginbottom lives?"

"No," she answered. "I've no idea. It's not far away, I'm sure of that—Kevin would sometimes telephone him and he would be downstairs in less than ten minutes."

To know that Higginbottom lived within ten minutes' motor-cycle ride of this house wasn't exactly a good indication, but the information might help, at some stage. Roger did not press her further, but stood up, and said firmly:

"You will let me know at once if Kevin comes back or telephones, or if anything at all strange or unusual happens, won't you?"

She nodded.

"You really must," Roger insisted. "You won't help by hiding him and he won't help himself by hiding. But you know that as well as I do." He held out his hand, unexpectedly. "For my part I'll let you know if we get any news, Mrs. Spray. And don't hesitate to call the Secretary at the Hampstead Cottage Hospital."

With quivering lips, she replied: "I won't."

"I'll let myself out," said Roger.

He went down the wooden stairs, more aware of the creaks

and squeaks which came from them. When he opened the door from the apartment he saw three men in the editorial section, including the bearded, long-haired one he had seen before. There was no doubt that their interest was in him; little, that he had been recognised. None of them spoke, and he went down and out into the street. A motor-cyclist with a crash helmet passed, motor roaring; the youth's face was so hidden by goggles that it wasn't even possible to be sure it was a youth; it could have been a girl, or a man of mature age. He walked with his customary briskness towards his car, and as he reached it a young man and a girl with a camera stepped out of a doorway.

"Mr. West!" the man called.

The girl raised and snapped the camera.

"Mr. West, may I ask what case has brought you to Mandeville Street?" The man had a flat voice and for a comparative youngster, very veined cheeks and bloodshot eyes. "I'm from the *Globe*. Name of Tweed."

"The *Globe* should know that when I've a statement to make I'll make it to all the Press," Roger said, amiably enough. He got into his car, and the girl bent down and took pictures of him through the window. He manoeuvred the car out of the parking place, drove a hundred yards or so, and then lifted the radio-telephone from its hook on the dashboard. *Information* answered almost at once.

"Two things," Roger said. "Have Division watch 29 Mandeville Street, Bloomsbury, in case young Spray turns up there. And have a patrol car pull up two people—a man who calls himself Tweed and says he's from the *Globe*, and a young woman with a camera—in Mandeville Street at this moment, and check who they are. I'm going back to the Yard. Let me know the result *en route*."

"Right, sir."

He drove into Holborn and then slowly along part of Oxford Street, as congested as he had ever known it; a swarming mass of people on either side of the road, already peering at the shops.

It was a little after eleven, he need not go back to the Yard yet unless he wanted to. The radio-telephone buzzed as he passed the end of New Bond Street, and he thought: that's quick work, as he lifted the receiver.

But it wasn't *Information:* it was his Detective Sergeant, Venables.

"What is it?" Roger demanded, and his thoughts changed swiftly to Sir Douglas Fellowes and the autopsy.

"The autopsy report's ready, sir. We haven't any copies yet but I've been able to establish one thing, which I thought you would like to know at once."

"What is it?" demanded Roger, and wondered: cancer or no cancer?

"He was a very healthy man, sir. No vestige of cancer. No non-malignant growths, either. Nothing to indicate why he should think he was grievously ill, sir. I did wonder—" Venables, a man of remarkable ability not yet always properly controlled, broke off, obviously uncertain whether he should have kept what he had wondered to himself.

"Well, let's have it," Roger said.

"Well, sir, the report hasn't even gone to the Home Office yet; I managed to get this information from the pathologist's secretary. And that means the family doesn't know yet. I—er—I thought perhaps—"

Roger let him flounder, guessing what was in his mind, sure that he would be well rewarded for his awkwardness and embarrassment if Roger declared it a good idea.

"Well, what I mean is, would it be a good thing for *you* to convey the news to Lady Fellowes?" Venables managed to say at last. "She would be taken completely unawares. Bit of a dirty trick, but—" His voice faded, and Roger could imagine him sitting at his desk, looking thoroughly miserable.

"Might be a very good idea," Roger conceded.

Venables's voice brightened. "You think so, sir?"

"Yes. Yes, I'll go and see her," Roger decided. "If the Commander wants me, tell him where I've gone."

"Like a shot!" crowed Venables. "By the way, sir—there's not a word about young Spray's friend Higginbottom at the University or at the rooms they share. Not a word."

He rang off and Roger replaced the receiver, and without conscious thought, changed his route. Sir Douglas Fellowes had lived in a block of luxury flats in Berkeley Square, and from here Roger need only make a detour of five minutes or so. If he were lucky, he might be able to talk to the new widow and get back to the Yard by mid-day, as Coppell had ordered. He had a traffic-free run but then had to drive twice round Berkeley Square before calling a constable and telling him to look after the car.

"And what is the best way to Rexham Towers?" he asked.

"It's that block over there, sir," replied the constable, pointing across the Square. "The garden gates are open, I'd walk across that way if I were you."

"Thanks," Roger said, and opened the nearest gate.

The garden was at its spring loveliest, with clusters of daffodils beneath some of the trees and in the central lawn, where toddlers played and, even in this day and age, nursemaids sat with their charges, and gossiped. He walked more slowly, partly because of the quietness and the beauty of this sylvan oasis in the heart of Mayfair, partly because he had to decide what approach to make to Lady Fellowes. He was almost sorry when he reached the other side of the garden, squeezed between two parked cars, a Bentley and an M.G.—the M.G. reminding him of Professor Clayton.

Cars were moving much too fast beyond the parked cars; one came so close that he jumped the last two feet. He glowered round at the car but had no time to take its number, then crossed the pavement and entered Rexham Towers. A tall doorman in a dark blue uniform approached.

"I'm afraid Lady Fellowes isn't seeing anybody, sir," this man told him. "You can leave a message. I—oh, *police* . . . Well in that case, I'll telephone and say you want to see her. Her daughter-in-law is with her," he confided as he reached a wall telephone in two long strides.

He explained, and turned to Roger as he put the receiver down.

"It's all right for you to go up, sir, the number's 79, on the seventh floor. Mrs. Fellowes says please don't keep her ladyship too long."

"Not a moment longer than I must," Roger promised as he stepped into a lift.

Before the doors closed, before he had any idea what was happening, there was a burst of activity and a young couple raced across the lobby and into the lift as the doorman bellowed: "No you don't!" The automatic lift doors closed as the girl of the couple pulled the strap of her camera free, while the rather plump young man who had been in Mandeville Street stood breathless but beaming with triumph as he asked:

"Do you think these two jobs are connected, Handsome?"

"If you make a nuisance of yourselves while I'm on a case I'll find a way of making you wish you hadn't," Roger said gruffly. "Have you been questioned by my men?"

"Oh, yes, and satisfied them that we work for the *Globe*," Tweed replied. "You wouldn't threaten the freedom of the Press, Mr. West, would you?"

"I'd put you on a charge of loitering if I thought you were threatening the effectiveness of a police inquiry," Roger replied sharply.

He knew that he might be over-reacting, but was far from sure, even when the young man said almost plaintively: "Oh, come, Handsome, you wouldn't do that, would you?"

8

Lady Fellowes

It was never wise to be deliberately hostile to the Press, and Roger fought back irritation at being called by his nickname by this young pup. He schooled himself to show no reaction to such questions, and remarked:

"I would do what I had to do. Meanwhile, be careful. That doorman could break your neck with one hand."

"But he won't," the newspaperman said, confidently.

"I shouldn't be too sure."

"You haven't said whether you think the two jobs are connected," the other said, accusingly.

"When you've been at this job a little longer, you'll know that policemen never answer questions if they can avoid it, and certainly never express opinions. But they do make statements. Your premise is wrong."

"Come again."

"The attack on Professor Clayton might be classified as a 'job'. The suicide of Sir Douglas Fellowes certainly couldn't. I—"

The lift stopped, the doors opened, and the tall doorman, now looking both huge and menacing, appeared by some miracle at the widening gap. He eased to one side enough to allow Roger to pass, repeated: "No you don't," to the others and thrust the *Globe* reporter back into the lift car with great and deliberate vigour. Roger glanced round long enough to see the doorman disappearing into the lift, arms outspread to make sure the others did not get past them. The doors began to close.

This was a wide, carpeted passage, with elaborate light fittings, paintings or good facsimiles of paintings on the panelled walls, doors on either side with the number on each in black lettering on avocado green. The whole place had an air of opulence. He passed number 71, found the next was 73 and so knew he was heading in the right direction; he stopped for a moment outside number 79. A bell push was at one side. He was vividly aware of going to see Ida Spray, and as vividly aware of the newspaperman's question. The two affairs *couldn't* be connected, could they?

Almost as soon as he pressed the bell, the door opened.

A young woman, little more than a girl, appeared, looking at him soberly. She had long hair, golden-coloured, brushed straight down to her shoulders, and wore a mini-skirted dress. In her way she was beautifully turned out, and her grey eyes were quite lovely.

"Are you Superintendent West?"

"Yes," Roger said.

"Please do come in." She stood aside. "You won't harass my mother too much, will you?"

Was this daughter or daughter-in-law? Was she old enough to be married?

"I shall try not to," he said.

"She is so terribly upset."

"I'm sure she is. Are you—"

"I'm Helen Fellowes."

"Mrs. Fellowes?"

"Yes."

"Would you care to be present while I'm with your mother?"

"Very much," Helen Fellowes said in her most assured manner. "Thank you." He found her protracted gaze a little disconcerting; it was almost as if she were looking for some special message in his expression, but at last she looked and turned away.

There was a large, square hallway with doors leading off on both sides and at the far end; just one, at the end, opposite the front door. Helen Fellowes went straight to this, which stood ajar, and announced quietly to whoever was beyond:

"It's Superintendent West, mummy."

She stood aside for Roger to enter and find Lady Fellowes alone in a long, beautiful room. The decor was blue and dove grey, with wide windows overlooking the Square; Roger's feet sank into luxurious carpet, but it was the woman who caught and held his attention. She was in pale grey; her hair was grey, and fell about her shoulders, like the girl's. She had an absolutely colourless but startlingly beautiful face. He did not know why the word occurred to him but he thought she was a tragic Madonna.

She moved towards him from an open writing desk, a French escritoire with painted panels.

"Superintendent," she said, "how can I help you?"

My God, what eyes!

"Lady Fellowes," he replied, "I have had an early notice of the post mortem report on your husband, and I wanted to come and tell you the result myself." He paused deliberately for a few moments, and then went on: "There was no indication of cancer whatsoever."

She didn't respond; did not speak or move. But the girl moved past Roger to the older woman's side.

"And since your husband held a position of such importance I have been assigned to the task of finding out if there was any other different reason for his action." He felt positive that plain words, without frills, were necessary here. Both of these women would see through any kind of pretence on the instant.

Neither of them spoke.

"Clearly, there could be a strong personal and emotional

67

reason," Roger went on. "As clearly, there is the possibility that some pressure was brought to bear on him over the Common Market, some—"

Lady Fellowes said: "Please don't go on."

"Lady Fellowes," said Roger. "Sooner or later I have to go on. Isn't it better sooner than later?" When she didn't answer he asked: "Have you seen this morning's *Daily Globe*?"

"That rag!" exclaimed Helen.

"Yes," Lady Fellowes answered. "Our friends made sure that we saw the newspaper." She seemed to unfreeze, moved, and indicated a chair. "Please sit down, Mr. West. Helen, I'm sure Mr. West would like some coffee, and I think perhaps I would, too."

Roger sat down, aware of the crossed glances of the two women; the younger one, hesitant, doubtful; the other, commanding. It was only a brief conflict, ending when Helen smiled, turned and said: "Of course." What had that been about? Roger wondered. He settled back in a Regency winged armchair, a trifle too narrow for him at the shoulders. Was the woman going to stand? To his surprise, she pulled up a brocade-covered pouffe and sat on that, crossing her hands in her lap. She moved beautifully. As she did these things she looked out of the window, at some photographs on a Bechstein grand piano in a corner from which the keys and music rest had good window light, but finally at Roger.

"Mr. West," she said, "I suppose it is no use asking you to treat what I am going to say in confidence?"

"It will depend on what it is," Roger said, and after a pause added with obvious feeling: "I didn't like the article in the *Globe* either. No one at the Yard likes rumour, gossip or scandal, and anything you say would only be made public if it were clearly in the public interest."

Her eyes held a brighter light.

"You are very understanding. Mr. West, I did not for one moment think that my husband had, or feared that he had, cancer. I know, or I believe I know, why he killed himself. His note of explanation was an attempt to save me and our family from scandal and perhaps humiliation. My husband killed himself because he was being blackmailed. He had been, for over a year. I didn't know until after his death." She was speaking in short sentences and pausing noticeably between each one, as asthmatics did sometimes, and some under great emotional stress. "My son and his wife knew. I heard them discussing it not long after I was told of his—my husband's—death. I am sure they would not have told me, otherwise. But I was insistent. I had to be told all. My husband had been blackmailed for over a year because he kept the fact that he had a mistress unknown to me. He committed suicide because he could no longer go on paying for silence. And because—" Now she gulped, as if the words choked her. "And because he was afraid of what I would do if I found out."

She sat on the pouffe, ankles crossed, legs at one side, hands still in her lap. Her eyes burned—as Ida Spray's had, only an hour or so ago. Roger was acutely aware of the intensity of her gaze, but that was not all. He was suffering from the shock of learning that the cause had been blackmail.

The plump face of the *Globe* man hovered in front of Roger's mind's eye, and his voice seemed to echo in Roger's ears.

"Do you think these two jobs are connected, Handsome?"

Blackmail of a man who had been deceiving his wife for years and was afraid of being found out.

He fought back the dozens of questions which sprang to his mind as he looked into Lady Fellowes's eyes. Their brilliance was such that they looked like silver; silver, caught by the sun.

She said: "So you see, in a way I killed him."

Roger started.

She went on with weariness: "But you don't see, do you? I thought for a moment that you would." The silvery light faded, the eyes became dull.

Roger exploded: "Nonsense!"

"I beg your pardon?" She was startled.

"Absolute nonsense," Roger insisted. "Convention may have killed him. Fear of what his friends and colleagues might think, but—he killed himself, Lady Fellowes. There isn't a shadow of doubt about that. A man is responsible for his own actions, no one else is responsible for them."

She looked astounded.

"No part of my job to moralise," Roger went on gruffly. "But—it is true, you know. Will you answer me one question?"

Still astonished, almost dazed, she answered: "If I can."

"If your husband had told you the truth what would you have done?"

She closed her eyes.

He wondered if he had gone too far, whether he could justify his attitude or his actions. He could, to himself. He wanted to get her to talk fully and freely, and believed that if she continued with the belief that she was responsible, she would keep her mind half-closed. He was aware of a faint sound at the door but did not glance round, and Lady Fellowes seemed unaware of it.

Her eyes were still closed.

If her answer was that she would have left her husband; divorced him; caused the scandal he had so feared, then obviously she did carry a share of the responsibility and she would never refuse to admit it. What was going on in her mind? What tormented thoughts?

She opened her eyes.

"I would have told him that for years past I also have had a lover," she said.

He saw the tears fill her eyes; saw them spill slowly down her cheeks. Then the door opened wider and Helen came in with a laden tray, a bright-eyed Helen. He felt sure she had been at the door during those few minutes of 'confession'. She placed the tray on a table between Roger and her mother-in-law, and

70

looked at Roger so that the older woman could not see her. Her eyes glowed, she formed two words he could not mistake:

"Thank you. Oh, thank you."

Then, quite matter-of-factly, she began to pour out. There were biscuits and sandwiches on the tray, and she placed some on a small plate and put the plate in the other's hands.

"Cream and sugar, Mr. West?"

"A little of each, please . . . Thank you." He saw Lady Fellowes put a delicate-looking sandwich to her lips, and begin to eat, mechanically, drank coffee and had a biscuit before the older woman said:

"So you are not shocked, Mr. West?"

"I feel partly vindicated," Roger said, soberly. "The suicide isn't conceivably your fault. You must surely see that."

"I—I am beginning to. Helen has been trying to make me believe what you say, also." She smiled at her daughter-in-law. "How does this affect your inquiry, Mr. West?"

"Very much," he said. "I need to know everything I can about the blackmail, the amount paid, the method of collection—"

"Hubert—that is, my husband—knows more about that than anybody," Helen broke in. Her face was positively radiant. "And I know he'll give you all the help he can."

"Where is he?" asked Roger.

"He's at his office, in the city," Helen answered. "Would you like me to telephone him?"

"I'd like him to come and see me at Scotland Yard as soon as he can," Roger said, standing up. "Lady Fellowes, at this stage I don't see any reason at all for the facts to be made public, but you may find that some of the Press are difficult and persistent, and not above presenting rumour and guesswork in the guise of facts. One or two may come in here and worry you once the report on the autopsy is known, and it may be known before the inquest."

"Have you any advice for me?" asked Lady Fellowes. She

both looked and sounded more relaxed than at any time since Roger had arrived.

"It is not unknown for human beings to be convinced they have an incurable disease when in fact they are quite healthy," Roger said. He backed a pace, looking down on the beautiful face, aware of Helen studying him, and then he went on in a stronger, sterner voice: "There isn't the slightest possibility that there was a political cause, is there? You have not invented this story in an effort to make quite sure we don't probe into his official activities, have you, Lady Fellowes?"

It seemed a long time before Helen gasped:

"What an awful thing to say!"

"I am simply trying to get at the truth," Roger replied, "and I am sorry if it causes you distress or pain. But your husband was deeply involved in political aspects of the Common Market, wasn't he? He traveled widely in Britain's interest, and—I simply have to be sure there is no hidden motive."

9

Truth?

It was some time after Helen's protest and Roger's comments before Lady Fellowes replied; then it was quietly, the words accompanied by a smile which seemed to play about the corners of her lips. She looked at him steadily.

"No," she said. "I have told you the truth, Mr. West. I am sure my son will confirm it, and will give you all the help he can. And"—the smile deepened—"that was the kind of question my husband would have asked. I don't mind how deeply you probe, provided you find the blackmailers."

"There we really have the men responsible for the suicide," Roger said. "Thank you very much." He turned and went towards the door, catching Helen unawares, but she sprang forward and opened it, stepping out into the hallway just behind him.

"Superintendent," she said.

"Yes, Mrs. Fellowes?"

"You won't—you won't harass Lady Fellowes more than you must, will you?"

Roger said, with the hard note in his voice: "Only as much as is necessary to find out the whole truth."

"You know the truth where my father-in-law is concerned," Helen assured him. "The absolute truth. There was never a more upright man, no one with greater integrity in his work."

"That's what I've been given to understand," Roger said. "Goodbye."

"I'll call my husband at once."

Husband! She was absurdly young to be married. The thought brought a smile to his eyes and, although she could not know what caused his, an answering smile to hers. She put out her hand; her grip was firm, her hand cool. He went out into the passage and to the lift. It would not have surprised him to find the *Globe* man and his girl photographer hovering, but they were not, although the doorman wasn't there. Roger walked across the garden again. The nursemaids had gone, with their prams and charges; some older people walked dogs and two girls sat amid daffodils, eating sandwiches from cellophane wrapping. As he stepped out of the far gate, Roger looked at his watch—it was twelve-twenty. As he glanced up the policeman with whom he had left the car came hurrying.

Trouble?

"Will you call your office at once, sir, please?"

"Yes," Roger said.

He guessed what Venables had to say; that Coppell was screaming for him. With the news he had, however, Coppell would soon calm down. He sat at the wheel and lifted the radio-telephone; in a moment he was talking to Venables.

"I thought you should know about this at once, sir," Venables said; so it wasn't Coppell. "Young Kevin Spray has been picked up."

"Where?" asked Roger, his interest quickened by a tone in the sergeant's voice.

"At Harwich, sir—where he was going on board the morning ferry to The Hague, with his Hokki. He was on the run all right, and"—that note, almost portentous and even ominous, grew deeper in Venables's tone—"there's blood on his Hokki motorcycle, although it's been washed. A few spots were left on the underneath of the mudguards and the petrol tank. The Harwich police want to know whether we'd like them to test for the blood

74

group, or send him to London with the machine and have the job done here."

Roger, ever watchful of the feelings of police in the provinces, answered at once, even as he digested this new piece of information.

"Ask Harwich to do a test, and then send them both back."

"They *did* ask if we'd like to send someone up to fetch the lad," Venables said.

"If they can spare a man I'd rather they sent him," decided Roger, and as he was about to ring off, he thought again of Coppell. "Any word from the Commander?"

"I gave him your message, sir," replied Venables. "He asked you to go and see him as soon as you got in. I assured him it would be before lunch."

"I'm on my way," Roger said. "Meanwhile, have Lady Fellowes's place watched and have her trailed wherever she goes."

He rang off on Venables's "Very good, sir," surprised at how heavy-hearted he felt, then suddenly exasperated with himself because he had forgotten to ask whether Kevin Spray had been alone. Venables would surely have reported had there been two motor-cyclists, however. He nodded, gave the helpful constable a preoccupied smile, and started the engine. The constable held up traffic until he was on the move. He drove with studied concentration, as he always did when he had a great deal to think about; preoccupation could lead to carelessness. Soon, he was back in New Bond Street and heading for Piccadilly, cut across to Pall Mall with the lights favouring him, and was at the Yard in twenty minutes, good going in the rush hour traffic. He left his car with a detective officer to take to the underground garage beneath the new building, and went up to his floor, glancing into Venables's office first. The sergeant, who looked tall and somehow clumsy even when sitting down, banged his knee beneath his desk as he started to get up. He winced.

"Any message from a Mr. Hubert Fellowes?" asked Roger.

75

"No, sir," answered Venables, giving his knee a surreptitious rub. "But the Commander rang only five minutes ago, sir—he's getting very anxious to see you."

That was probably the understatement of the year!

"I'll go along to his office," Roger said. "If Mr. Fellowes calls, I'll see him any time—the sooner the better, and I don't mind missing lunch."

"Right, sir."

Roger strode along to the Commander's office, which was at the other end of this passage. He tapped on the door marked *Commander, C.I.D.*, and Coppell roared: "Come in!" Roger opened the door, and was startled to see the Assistant Commissioner, Colonel Frobisher, a newly-appointed, lantern-jawed man, sitting by Coppell's desk.

"It's about time," Coppell said, rasping. "What's this about Professor Clayton coming to see you here last night?"

"He came to see any senior officer and I happened to be here," Roger replied. "Good morning, sir." He looked at the A.C. who replied in a rather high-pitched voice: "Good morning."

"I want you to concentrate on the three suicides," Coppell said. "Didn't I make that clear enough?"

"Yes," Roger answered. It was no use taking umbrage because Coppell was calling him down in front of another senior official. "And I'm doing so, sir."

"The *Clayton* case?"

"Commander," Roger said. "Sir Douglas Fellowes did not commit suicide because he thought he was ill, nor for any political reason. According to his wife, he was being blackmailed because he had a mistress. So was Professor Clayton. The motivation is so similar I think we should consider the possibility that they are associated. I'm quite sure," he added, as Coppell sat with his mouth agape and his hands gripping the arms of his chair. "I've just come from Lady Fellowes, who made her statement in confidence, and her daughter-in-law confirmed it. I am due to see her son, who is believed to know more details, in the next half-hour or so."

"Well—I'm—damned!" Coppell gasped, and then he turned to the Colonel and said gustily: "You see? Just as I told you. You think you've got Handsome West by the short hairs, and he gets away."

The A.C. gave a droll smile as he nodded.

"I see exactly what you mean. What about the other two suicides, Superintendent? Might they also be to do with the same case?" He was relaxed and somehow reassuring; likeable, too.

"I don't yet know, sir."

"And Aker may not have killed himself," Coppell said. He had recovered quickly and was frowning, almost scowling, causing a deep groove between his eyes. "Do you have any other reason for thinking the cases might be connected?"

"Not positively," answered Roger, "but Fellowes was in Australia about a year ago, and so was Clayton. More by luck than judgment that I found out, I'm afraid."

"We need more of that luck," observed the Assistant Commissioner. "The article in the *Globe* caused a great deal of anxiety in high government levels. We need to know exactly what is happening so as to prove conclusively that there is no kind of political motivation."

Roger looked at him steadily, vividly mindful of his last question to Lady Fellowes. Coppell also stayed silent, as if sensing that an issue had arisen between the Superintendent and the Assistant Commissioner, and he would be wise to keep out of it. In Roger's eyes there was a cold, calculating look; he had suddenly become fine-drawn and very intent. The Assistant Commissioner sat upright in a chair with leather padded arms and seat; curiously defensive.

"What political motivation is suspected?" Roger demanded at last. "What is being kept back from us, sir? If we don't know everything, our job is much more difficult than it need be. Was Sir Douglas suspected of some kind of double dealing?"

The Assistant Commissioner replied quietly: "The possibility is considered—no one is suspect."

"Possibility of what, sir?"

"Giving advance information about Britain's conditions for extending the Common Market to Commonwealth nations," answered Frobisher. "This possibility is being canvassed—so is the possibility that powerful groups in this country want to get us out at all costs. One way would be creating an issue by demanding entry of the Commonwealth, which Germany and France would certainly not allow. If the man organising such a movement were Sir Douglas Fellowes, then he would be extremely vulnerable to blackmail, and might prefer death to exposure. Are you absolutely sure the real trouble was domestic?"

"As nearly sure as I can be so far," Roger answered. "I expect to have convincing proof when I've talked to the dead man's son."

"I want to know the moment you've talked to him," delcared Coppell, unable to stay silent any longer.

The Assistant Commissioner simply nodded.

Hubert Fellowes, at the age of twenty-six, had the knowledge, experience and the appearance of a man ten years older, and so much more mature than his years. He was startlingly like his mother, and his once jet black hair was beginning to grey prematurely. He was tall and lean, and moved with rare grace for a man; just as there was something slightly feline about his mother so there was something pantherish about him.

"Yes, darling," he said into the telephone to Helen. "I'll go to see this man West at once."

"You can safely tell him everything," Helen said.

"He seems to have made a double conquest, you and mother at one swoop," Hubert remarked with an undertone of laughter.

"Don't worry, pet. I won't keep anything back. I'll call you as soon as I've seen him."

He rang off, and stood up from his desk.

He had a small office in an old building near the Stock Exchange, with a desk squeezed into a corner by the window. Six other offices, partitioned off what had been a long, wide passage, were between him and the entrance to this fifth floor, where the old-fashioned plug-in type telephone exchange was manned by the receptionist—at this particular one, an over made-up blonde.

"Do you know what time you'll be back, Mr. Fellowes?" she asked.

"Not until half-past three at the earliest," he said, and went out.

The car of an old-type open-faced lift passed, going down, and rather than wait for it to return he ran down the stairs. He could go out of the main doors into Threadneedle Street, or by a side door into a narrow alley which led to the private parking area where he kept his motor-cycle—a medium-sized Raleigh.

He went along the alley, past old stone walls, on uneven paving stones.

No one else was in sight; this was a short cut to nowhere except the car park. He reached this area, uneven with big cobble stones, and headed for the motor-cycle. As he cocked a leg over it, two small men appeared from behind a car, and rushed at him.

He first heard, then saw them, and felt a flare of alarm.

He tried to withdraw his leg, but the turn-up of his trousers caught in the saddle, and he was helplessly off-balance when they reached him. They wore crash helmets and goggles; all he noticed except for this was a tightness at the corners of one man's lips.

Each carried a bar of iron.

"Help!" he shouted. "Help!" But his voice hardly sounded, and suddenly the two men were striking at his bare head. Blood spread. He felt agonising pain in his head and in his neck. He tried to cover his head and face with his arms, but two blows seemed to break the bones, and more showered on his head until more blood appeared and he lost consciousness.

The two men turned and left him, still caught by the handlebars, head on the cobbles, face deathly pale; he hardly seemed to be breathing. Quiet settled on the parking place, broken by the distant sound of traffic and, closer by, the staccato roar of motor-cycle engines.

Roger looked into Venables's room, but for once the sergeant was not at his desk. He went into his own office, expecting to see the time of an appointment for young Hubert Fellowes on top of a pile; there was none. He frowned. Venables wouldn't forget, so it could only mean that Fellowes had not called. He glanced at a small electric wall-clock which had a very white face; it was nearly twenty-to-two; much later than he had expected. On the other hand he was impatient because news was so vital.

Wasn't it a vital matter to Fellowes's son, also?

He decided to wait until two o'clock before checking with Helen, and opened the Aker and the Gooden file. There was no longer any doubt; he must probe into the love-life of each man, and mustn't lose much time. In an ordinary inquiry he would have sent Venables or another sergeant, possibly an inspector. But he wanted to see this through himself. What kind of response would anyone else have got from Lady Fellowes, for instance?

Sir Jeremy Gooden's offices were in Lombard Street, not far from young Fellowes. A secretary there might be able to give him some information. He put in a call, and was soon speaking to a woman with a very gruff voice: if she hadn't called herself Mrs. Spooner he would have thought she was a man.

"Yes, I was Sir Jeremy's personal secretary . . . Yes, if you consider it necessary I can see you this afternoon . . . Three-thirty would be the best time for me . . . Very well, Mr. West."

Roger rang off, with a feeling that he had been put in his place; he smiled faintly, then pulled a copy of an A.A. Tour Book towards him. Aker had an apartment somewhere between London and the small private airfield where he did much of his experimental work. The airfield, in Surrey, was at least an hour's drive away.

"No chance of getting out there until everyone's gone home," Roger decided. "Shall I go first thing tomorrow, or send Venables?" He had not made up his mind when the outside telephone began to ring, and he lifted it briskly.

"Yes?"

"There's a Mrs. Fellowes on the line, sir," the operator said. "She says she must speak to you."

"Put her through," ordered Roger. Was this a brush-off? Or was Hubert Fellowes already out of his office? These questions came very quickly before Helen Fellowes spoke in an agitated voice.

"Hubert's been attacked," she stated with forced calm. "He's been taken to Charing Cross Hospital. I am going there at once."

Almost as a reflex action, Roger said:

"I'll be there nearly as soon as you are."

But she rang off so quickly that he wasn't sure she heard.

10

Second Victim

Suddenly, there were a dozen things to do at once.

Ring for Venables, who was out of his office, remember; call *Information* to check what they knew of the attack; call City Police, who would be in charge of the investigation; tell Coppell. As *Information* answered the communicating door opened and Venables appeared, head bent low to avoid the lintel, shoulders rounded, expression on his usually lugubrious face eager.

"We've just heard that Hubert Fellowes was attacked and found in a car park behind Threadneedle Street," *Information* said. "Two motor-cyclists were seen by one of the City officers to leave only ten minutes before a motorist who went there to park found him."

"I'm going first to the hospital, then to the place where it happened," said Roger. "Will you tell City?"

"Yes, sir."

"Thanks." Roger rang off and looked up at his sergeant. "Hubert, the son of Sir Douglas, was to give me some information about his father's *affaire* with another woman, and he's been attacked in a car park behind his office, apparently by two motor-cyclists. His wife called him at his office and told him to come and see me, so he was being watched, someone at the switchboard gave information away, or he himself told a third party. Take two men to City, ask their help, and find out all you can."

"Right, sir."

"The office is at—"

"I know it, sir," said Venables, who had a genius for knowing what would be wanted of him next.

"Then get going. I'll be at Charing Cross Hospital, then the car park, then at Gooden's offices in—"

"Lombard Street, sir?"

"One day he'll be too clever for his boots," Roger growled under his breath, but he nodded and made no comment. As Venables disappeared Roger rang for a car and driver to be downstairs for him; this was no occasion to have parking anxieties. Next he rang Coppell, whose secretary answered.

"The Commander won't be back for at least an hour, sir."

"Tell him Sir Douglas Fellowes's son has been attacked and I'm on that job," Roger said. "I'll report as soon as I can." He rang off and then picked up his 'murder bag', a box-like case not unlike a doctor's, which held all he would need at the scene of a crime. The City Police would have this well under control but it was wiser to go prepared for fresh trouble. He felt bothered by some factor he couldn't place—something he had overlooked, or at least wanted to think about.

His car, the Rover 3½ litre, was outside the Victoria Street entrance of the Yard, a detective officer standing by it.

"'Afternoon, Jones," Roger said. "Charing Cross Hospital, and wait for me."

"Very good, sir."

Roger sat back in the car, and for a few moments actually closed his eyes. The pressure had built up so suddenly, as it often did, that he felt as if he had been running, and had come to a standstill. He had a hazy kind of headache and faint nausea in his stomach; only then did he realise that he hadn't had lunch. He leaned forward.

"Pull in where you can and get me some fruit—from a barrow boy will do."

"No lunch, sir?" Jones didn't turn his head.

83

"No time," Roger replied.

"I know just the place," declared Jones. He took a left turn into a narrow street, then into a cul-de-sac, where no cars were parked. At the far end was a café with fruit and sandwiches piled in a narrow window. Jones parked half on the pavement, and got out smartly. In a very few minutes, while Roger sat back and allowed thoughts to drift through his mind, the driver returned with two apples, a pear and some ham sandwiches, all in cellophane bags.

"Thanks," Roger said warmly. "How much?"

"Eight shillings, sir—or forty new pence."

Roger paid what he still thought of as two shilling pieces, and sat back. The sandwiches were fresh, and enjoyable; he found himself 'seeing' those on the tray at Lady Fellowes's flat. Ah! That was what troubled him; he should have placed a close watch on Lady Fellowes and her daughter-in-law Helen, there was no way of being sure of the motive for the attack on Hubert, no way of being certain his mother and his wife were not in danger.

Roger sent an order through to the Yard, to have the two women and the flat watched, then sat back to finish his snack. He was trying to stop juice from the pear drooling down his chin as they turned into the forecourt of the hospital, which was tucked away behind St. Martin's-in-the-Field. He thrust a sticky handkerchief into his trousers pocket as he entered the hospital. Two young porters were sparring behind the reception desk, but swung towards him immediately, one blond, one almost black-haired and black-skinned.

"Help you, sir?"

Roger showed his card. "I want to see Mr. Fellowes," he said.

"You won't be able to do that," the young Jamaican said. "He's in surgery."

"His wife's with the matron of Accident Ward," volunteered the other. "Shall I take you up, sir?"

"Please."

Hospitals looked the same, smelled the same; sharply antiseptic. Roger's mouth felt tacky and dry as he went along with the blond young man. They turned into a small room where Helen Fellowes was sitting with a small sharp-featured woman in a blue gown: the Matron.

Roger saw Helen's head turn.

"I can't tell you how sorry I am," he said. "How is he?"

"Who—" began the Matron.

"Superintendent West of New Scotland Yard," breathed the porter.

"No one will tell me, only that he is being operated on and it is very serious," Helen replied. Her voice was steady and she was dry-eyed but very pale. "Do you know what happened?"

"I'm on my way to find out," Roger said. "What can you tell me?"

"Only that I telephoned him and he promised to come and see you as soon as he could."

"Where was he when you spoke to him?"

"At his office."

"He couldn't have been at a restaurant, or—"

"Of course not," interrupted Helen impatiently. "I called him at his office."

"On a direct line?"

"No, through the office exchange. He has no direct—" She broke off with a gasp, as if suddenly realising what Roger was driving at. She leaned back in a tubular steel armchair, staring at him, and for the first time the Matron moved so that Roger could see her. The porter had gone. "You mean, someone may have—have talked about where he was coming?"

"Yes," Roger said.

"Mr. West," the Matron said at last. "Mrs. Fellowes is already suffering from a great strain. I do hope you won't make it any worse."

"Be sure that I'll try not to," Roger replied, and went on to Helen: "Do you know if your husband had a confidante at the office, Mrs. Fellowes?"

"He wouldn't confide in anyone about—about this," Helen said. "I'm absolutely sure."

She could be wrong, but she was obviously sure she was right and there was no point in asking questions about that.

"Does Lady Fellowes know?" he inquired.

"Yes."

"Is anyone with her?"

"Yes," answered Helen. "And I shall telephone as soon as there is news."

"The moment we have word from the operating theatre, we will tell Mrs. Fellowes," the Matron put in.

"And please telephone me—and leave a message if I'm not in my office." Roger gave her a card as he stood up, turned to the girl and repeated: "I can't tell you how sorry I am."

There were tears in her eyes as she nodded.

Roger went out, more shaken in a way than when he had gone in; seeing the girl had made the tragedy so much more vivid. And a measure of the responsibility was his. He had asked her to telephone her husband, and Hubert Fellowes had been attacked before he could get to the Yard. Surely the attack had been to stop him; what other possible reason could there be?

The car and Jones were waiting for him; the two porters watched from the main doors.

"Number 1181 Throgmorton Street," Roger ordered. "Do you know the parking place just behind it?"

"I'll soon find it," Jones said.

In fact it was easy, for two uniformed City policemen with the City crown on their helmets were on duty by the narrow entry road; until they realised it was a police car, they refused entry. Soon, Roger stepped out into a cobbled courtyard hemmed in by tall buildings. At one side was a heavy motor-cycle, with chalk marks alongside it—marks which indicated where the victim of

86

the affair had lain. Several plainclothes men from the City police were examining some marks on the cobbles, and Venables was with them.

"Any luck?" Roger asked generally.

Venables started and one of the others straightened up slowly; he was an Inspector and an old acquaintance of Roger, a greying man with a very thin face and very thin lips which curved into a surprisingly attractive smile.

"Your sergeant had us looking for motor-cyclists," he remarked.

"Find any?" asked Roger, nodding to Venables.

"Some have been here and we've several sets of tyre prints," the City man replied. "And we've found three different passers-by who say they saw two motor-cycles go off about the time of the attack."

"Sir," said Venables.

"Well?"

"Some Japanese tyre prints made for Hokki motor-cycles were isolated at the Hampstead house this morning," Venables reported. "So if these prints are the same we may have made a good start."

"You concentrate on them," Roger ordered, and was rewarded by a flash of a smile from thick lips. "Keep me in touch at the office." He turned to the City man. "I've another job I'd like to do upstairs; can you spare a few minutes?"

"Of course." The City man, whose name was Pilkington, moved with him along the narrow road. Neither officer found the situation strange although there was strangeness in it, for the City of London Police covered a small area in the heart of Metropolitan London, quite separate from the area covered by the Metropolitan Police; when investigations overlapped, the two forces worked closely together; but here, the Inspector was officially in charge; Roger, though senior in rank, was not able to direct any course of action.

"What's on?" asked Pilkington.

"I think that someone in Hubert Fellowes's office overheard his conversation with his wife when she asked him to come and see me," Roger said.

"And set out to stop him?" Pilkington flashed.

"Possibly."

"Who—"

"It could be the telephone operator. It could be someone in whom Fellowes confided," Roger said. "Will you check it?"

"Like a shot," agreed Pilkington. "But—" He paused as they reached the front entrance of the building.

"But what?" asked Roger.

"If you're right, and if the attack was made by two motor-cyclists, then they were pretty close by to get here in time."

"Yes," agreed Roger. "I don't know the exact timing yet, and I do know that it seems unlikely. But if you'll check, I'd like to get along and see someone else in your manor—but someone about whom we've been officially consulted."

"Sir Jeremy Gooden?" asked Pilkington.

"His secretary."

"Old battleaxe," Pilkington remarked. "I wish you luck. Will you come along to Old Jewry afterwards?"

"That, or telephone," Roger said.

"Look in if you can," urged Pilkington, which was his way of saying that the City Police would like him to visit their headquarters in person; it was, in its way, a very real compliment.

Pilkington went into the building. Jones was standing by, and he asked: "Shall I get the car, sir?"

"I'm going to Gooden's office in Throgmorton Street," said Roger, "and I'll walk, but you get there in the car as soon as you can."

"Very good, sir."

Jones went off, and Roger found himself walking with a stream of people towards Throgmorton Street. It was difficult to hurry, the crowd was so thick, but as far as he knew there was nothing happening to draw them. Soon, he was able to cut through an alley and another courtyard to the street he wanted, and was close to the Gooden office. He found this to be a fairly small but modern building, jammed between much older ones. On the noticeboard by the two lifts was a list of occupants; Gooden and Lynch, Commercial Bankers, were on the fifth of seven floors. He stepped out of the lift onto a reception area, where a young woman who was beautifully turned out sat at a large desk.

"Good afternoon, sir. May I help you?"

"I've an appointment with Mrs. Spooner," Roger said.

The young woman gave a considered smile. "Are you Chief Detective Superintendent West?"

Roger couldn't resist saying: "*Roger* West."

"Chief Detective Superintendent *Roger* West, thank you, sir. I will tell Mrs. Spooner you are here."

She turned to an ultra-modern press button telephone exchange and pressed a button, announced Roger, and then said: "Yes, Mrs. Spooner." She turned to Roger. "If you will go through the swing doors and turn right, Mrs. *Elizabeth* Spooner will meet you."

She had grey eyes, which twinkled.

Roger's twinkled back.

Then he went through the swing doors, wondering what the 'old battleaxe' would be like. A long passage, with several doors leading off, was empty until he was halfway along, when a woman turned the far corner and came towards him. She was tall, and wore grey hair in a severe Eton crop. She wore a dark green suit with a calf-length skirt which surely came from the days when women's suits were called costumes. She approached with a curiously one-sided walk, and he thought, 'battleship, not battleaxe'. She gripped his hand with one considerably larger, and said: "You are very prompt" in her unmistakable voice, and led him into a room at the far end of the passage: obviously, her office. He had an impression of spaciousness, but before Roger could take in the room or indeed the woman, she closed the door and went on aggressively: "I don't know what you've been up to, Superintendent, but since you called *I've* been threatened with a violent death if I talk to you."

11

"Battleaxe"

They stood facing each other, a few feet apart.

The 'old battleaxe' now looked exactly what Pilkington had called her. She had a massive jaw and a small, thin mouth. Her skin had the very lined and leathery look of someone well into her sixties. Her nose was broad at base and bridge; broken, probably early in youth; but for her huge but well-confined bosom, Roger would have thought she was a man. Her eyes were small and deepset; very bright blue.

"So you've been threatened with violent death if you talk to me," Roger said, quietly.

"Yes. Also—"

"What are you going to do about it?" Roger interrupted.

"What do you expect me to do?" She didn't ask him to sit down but stood with an aggressiveness rare in both man and woman; he had no idea what was actually going through her mind but he wasn't surprised at the effect she had on Pilkington.

Roger smiled, disarmingly.

"I expect you to tell me the truth—that Sir Jeremy killed himself because he was being blackmailed, possibly over a woman, not—"

"How the burning hades did you know *that?*" she cried.

There was satisfaction in having completely taken her off balance; she actually drew back a step. But such satisfaction was unimportant; what mattered was her admission; and in a way he was nearly as badly shaken as Elizabeth Spooner; it had seemed almost incredible that the cause of the third suicide should appear to be identical with the first two.

He answered: "It seems to be part of a pattern."

"To hell with that! Who told you?"

"Mrs. Spooner," Roger said stiffly. "I don't make a habit of lying. If any person told me, you did. This is the third suspected suicide I am investigating, and the other two are said to have had this motivation."

"So you took a shot in the dark," she grumbled.

"Yes. How long had the *affaire* been going on?"

"Ten years," answered Elizabeth Spooner, not yet mollified. "Sir Jeremy travelled a great deal on business, and his—lady friend—often went with him. They did not meet in London very much. She is abroad now," the woman added. "She collapsed at the news, and I persuaded her to go and stay with friends."

"I see," Roger said, heavily. He wanted to stick to the main issue, and asked: "And you think he was afraid of divorce and the resultant scandal if the truth came out?"

"Yes."

"Was he justified in his anxiety?"

"Probably. You'd better ask his wife."

"Were you aware of the extra-marital liaison?"

"Yes. I was Sir Jeremy's confidential secretary." She put just enough emphasis on the word 'confidential' to show that she was recovering her spirit.

"Do you know who was blackmailing him?"

"No."

"Why didn't you come to the police with the real explanation?"

"He did not wish me to."

"Did he tell you in advance that he was going to kill himself?"

"No. He left me a letter."

"And you respected his dying wish rather than help us find

the people who drove him to commit suicide," Roger said; he made it sound like an accusation.

"Yes," she said, flatly. "And I would again."

"Where is the letter now?"

"I destroyed it."

"Who threatened you just before I arrived?" Roger demanded, without any change in tone or expression; and she answered in the same way.

"A man."

"Did you recognise the voice?"

"Yes. The same man had telephoned Sir Jeremy several times."

"Could you identify the speaker?"

"No. But I would recognise the voice at any time."

"What exactly did the man say to you?"

"He said that I would probably have a visit from a Mr. Bloody Handsome West of Scotland Yard, and if I knew what was good for me, I would not give Bloody West any information."

"And what did you say?"

"Nothing. I hung up on him."

"Are you nervous of what might happen as a result?"

After a long pause, she answered quietly: "Yes, I am. I don't want to be knocked about. Do you think he was serious?"

"Yes," answered Roger, "although if he knows for certain that you've told me all you can, he may not make any attack—he may decide it's a waste of time." They hadn't left Clayton alone after his visit, though, but there was no point in alarming her. A new thought entered his head: neither Clayton nor young Fellowes had been actually killed; it was almost as if only their temporary silence mattered.

"So there have been others," Elizabeth Spooner breathed, and before Roger could speak, she went on: "What do you want me to do, Mr. West?"

"I would very much like you to dig far back in your memory,

to the time when you first had any reason to suspect that Sir Jeremy was being blackmailed, and write down every related incident which followed. The number of times this particular man telephoned, for instance, any confidences which Sir Jeremy placed in you about the problem. A complete history, in other words." She gave an almost imperceptible nod before he went on: "And before I leave I would like you to tell me all you can about his wife and family."

"He had no family," she answered at once. "Just his wife—the sister of one of the other partners in the firm. I think he was as much concerned about his brother-in-law as his wife. He would probably have been compelled to leave the firm." She raised her hands. "I cannot be sure about this but I think so."

"Will you do what I ask?" Roger said.

"Of course."

"And telephone my office the moment the man telephones again."

"Yes. Do you expect him to?"

"I expect him to call as soon as I'm gone," Roger told her, "and I expect him to ask you what you told me."

"Shall I tell him?"

"I think it would be best not to lie," Roger said, quietly. "From now on, of course, you will have full police protection until we've caught this man and any accomplices he may have."

She nodded, without comment.

When Roger left the offices, the perfectly groomed girl at the newest kind of telephone exchange gave him a smile with her lips as well as with her eyes; in her way, she was quite a beauty. He was at street level before he made himself put her out of his mind, for Jones was there, against a background of fast-walking people and slow-moving traffic.

"The car's just round the corner, sir."

"We'll go to Old Jewry," Roger decided. "It's not far, but I want to talk to City before I get there." He arrived at the City of London Police headquarters *via* Scotland Yard's Information

Room and asked simply for protection for Elizabeth Spooner. "I'll explain when I reach you," he went on, and then sat back in the car while Jones coped with traffic which was far thicker and smellier than when they had first arrived.

"A lorry got out of control up near Aldgate," Jones told him. "It's one-way traffic up near the pump."

"I'll walk. You get to me as soon as you can," Roger said.

It was not until one was in these narrow streets of the City, where the great banks and insurance companies and many of the commercial houses had their headquarters that one realised how overcrowded the streets were and how, on a still, airless day like this, one breathed in petrol fumes until one coughed and spluttered. Yet when he turned into a side street close to Old Jewry the crowd seemed to vanish and the air was cleaner. There was a public convenience a few yards along, and Roger nipped down the stone steps; few things were more exasperating than to have to rush to the men's room on arrival at a strange place. The place, nearly a hundred years old, was like a dungeon, but the only odour was strong disinfectant. An old gnome of a man appeared, carrying a bucket.

"Nice day, sir."

"Not too bad at all," Roger said, not sure whether to prefer the petrol fumes to the carbolic. He ran up the steps.

A shadow warned him.

A shadow appeared and then vanished, spherical in shape.

He slowed down a little, gripping the cold, iron handrail. Had it been imagination? He neared the top steps. Had anyone been about to come down they would have shown themselves by now. He reached the top and leapt forward, ready to feel a fool if he were wrong.

Two youths leapt at him, one from the kerb, one from the other side. Had he gone up at leisurely pace they would have been on him and he would have had no chance, but his swift move forward took them unawares, for a moment they were face to face, weapons raised high above their heads.

Roger could swing round, and counter attack.

Or he could run hell-for-leather, away from the danger.

He swung round, and crouched. The pair, wearing crash helmets and goggles, turned towards him, ready to rush into the attack. He leapt, as in a rugby tackle, arms widespread, then closing like a giant pair of calipers about the legs of the two youths. They wore heavy boots, and one got a leg free and kicked, catching Roger on the side of the head, hurting but not putting him out of action. He knew exactly what he wanted to do, and hugged three legs, then heaved so that the pair toppled backwards to the edge of the steps. He heaved again. A foot caught him on the ear, stinging, making his head ring, but it was accidental. They began to fall. He hooked their legs from under them and they went down, heads, shoulders, torsos disappearing, leather-booted feet waving. He straightened up, gasping for breath, heard a car engine, then heard the car grind to a standstill.

Rescuers for the two attackers.

Jones bellowed: "Leave them to me, sir!" It was the police car and driver Jones hurtled past Roger towards the head of the steps.

Roger saw him pause, and went forward.

One of the attackers lay at the bottom of the steps, body twisted in an odd position, neck bent at a strange angle. The other was picking himself up, slowly, easing his crash helmet off. His goggles were askew and he took them off. He *was* a youth, little more than a boy. He seemed dazed. Both Roger and Jones watched, while the gnome-like man appeared from his antiseptic cavern and stood staring.

"Tom," gasped the youth, going slowly forward. "Tom," he repeated brokenly, and he went down on one knee by the side of the other, taking off the gauntlet glove from his right hand. He felt for the fallen man's pulse with his forefinger, the right way, and for what seemed an age knelt absolutely still.

96

His young face when he spun round was so distorted that it was satyrish; his tongue stuck, pointed-tipped, as he spoke.

"You've killed him, you swine! Wait till I get at you, wait—" He went on and on, glaring up at Roger and backing away from his friend, who had not moved and certainly showed no sign of life. He mouthed threats and obscenities as he backed, obviously planning to get inside the convenience, where there was an emergency exit.

Roger felt a surge of alarm, for the gnome-like man.

"I'll go—" Jones began.

As he spoke, the attendant grabbed one of the youth's wrists and with a dextrous twist turned and thrust it up behind him. An obscene oath turned into a scream, and Jones rushed down, but the gnome needed no help, he had his prisoner in a grip from which there was no escape. Roger went down the steps more slowly than Jones, watching the man with the crooked neck.

If appearances told the truth, he was dead.

In half-an-hour, a great deal happened.

An ambulance came, with a police-surgeon, and pronounced the assailant dead of a broken neck. Three men came from City Police Headquarters, and took the prisoner off. Roger talked to *Information*, who would pass on his report to the Commander; and finally, Roger went to the H.Q., an old building with narrow stone steps and an atmosphere, but for the open doors, of a prison. The Superintendent-in-Charge came out of a small office to make Roger welcome, provide tea, offer something stronger.

"No thanks," Roger said. "Not now. I have to talk to the prisoner."

"From what they tell me, he won't say a word," the Superintendent observed. "Except threaten to kill you. They were actually lying in wait for you, were they?" When Roger nodded, the burly man asked shrewdly: "Have you discovered something someone doesn't want you to pass on?"

"That's what I need to find out. Did the prisoner give his name?"

"He called himself John Smith," answered the Superintendent. "And his left arm is full of hypodermic needle punctures. He's hopped up about as high as he can be." After a pause, Pilkington went on: "We've found two motor-cycles, both Hokkis, with their fingerprints all over them."

"Where?" asked Roger.

"In a car park round the corner, only a minute's walk away from here," Pilkington answered.

Roger went along to the cells to see the youth.

From a distance, he was a baby-faced boy with blue eyes; but as Roger drew nearer he saw the grey pallor of the skin, the tell-tale dullness of the eyes, all the signs of a young person on heroin; at sight of him the youth burst into a torrent of vituperation shocking even to the ears of men who had long worked with the dregs of humanity.

It wasn't simply that he would not answer questions: he shouted and raved and threw himself about, and simply would not listen. To Roger, it was like listening to a madman.

He noticed that this man had a badge, a Japanese form of H—for Hokki? The dead youth had also had one. A moment later he had a shattering thought: how many more such youths were there?

Could there possibly be only the two?

In a curiously depressed mood despite the captures, Roger left Old Jewry for Scotland Yard just before six o'clock. Jones, back at the car, had picked up no messages for him; so presumably Venables had come up with nothing of importance. Sitting next to Jones, with the thick of the evening rush-hour traffic nearly over, Roger was aware of a sore head and increasing anxiety. He called Venables on the radio-telephone.

"I was hoping you would call, sir," Venables said. "The tyre prints in the car park behind Mr. Fellowes's office were the same as the prints at Professor Clayton's. But they're *not* identical with prints made by the tyres of the two machines picked up in Aldgate."

"So there were probably four motor-cyclists at least," Roger said heavily.

"Well, sir, almost certainly four motor-cycles, all Hokkis."

Roger let the correction pass as he remarked slowly: "It could be a motor-cycle club."

"There are hundreds of them."

"Yes. How many Hokki clubs?"

"Plenty, I should say," answered Venables. "Shall I start working on clubs, sir?"

"Yes. We especially want clubs which have some members who take heroin," Roger told him. "We want—" He broke off. "You know what we want. How will you go about this?"

"Ask all London divisions for Hokki Club information by telephone, and take it from there," Venables answered. "There may be some information by the time you're back, sir."

Roger said: "I'm going home for an hour or two first. If anything turns up, call me there. And call me if I'm not in the office before you leave."

"Very good, sir," said Venables.

It was absurd to imagine a note of reproach in his voice, yet Roger fancied there was one. Venables, a bachelor in his late twenties, thought nothing of staying at the Yard all night and once or twice, by inference, had shown that he felt a policeman's first duty was to his job, not to his wife and family. And so it was. But there was no point now in leaving Janet on her own all the evening; no point in allowing tension to grow between them almost as soon as they had come back from a holiday intended to take away tensions which the demands of Roger's job created.

He glanced at Jones.

"Bell Street," he ordered. "I'll pick up my car later."

"Very good, sir," Jones said, matter-of-factly. He cut through to the Embankment at Blackfriars, and reached Chelsea a little before half-past six. As they turned the corner of Bell Street, a short thoroughfare of detached and semi-detached houses each with its own well-tended garden, he saw his son Richard appear at the front door of his house, looking up and down, presumably for him.

"Sorry," Roger said, leaning across Jones and touching the car horn.

Richard looked quickly towards the sound, then came hurrying to the pavement, tall, lean, dark-haired, strikingly good-looking, especially at a distance. His expression was more eager than anxious, and as the car pulled up he opened Roger's door, said: "Good evening, driver," and went on to Roger: "A Lady Fellowes is indoors, Dad, anxious to see you. Mother sent me out to give you some warning."

100

12

Hokki Club?

Roger stood by Richard's side, leaned down and told Jones he could go, and walked with his son up the crazy paving path which led to the front of the detached, yellow brick house, mellowed by the near-thirty years the Wests had lived there, with a beautifully-kept lawn and a matured garden.

Richard was saying: "She only got here about ten minutes ago. Apparently she had telephoned the Yard and they said you were on your way here. She's stunning, isn't she?"

"How much has she said?"

"Very little. Mum offered her a drink and they're in the front room—*her* back's to the window, so just keep your voice down. She just said it was extremely urgent that she should talk to you."

"Confidentially."

"Good Lord! Yes." Richard's bright eyes flashed; he could behave as if he were the most naive young man in the world; although in some ways he was most sophisticated. "What's on, Dad?"

"Her husband died two days ago and her only son was brutally attacked this lunch-time, and may be dead."

"Good Lord!" exclaimed Richard again. "You'd think she hadn't a care in the world. Er—can I help?"

"Have you got your car here?"

"Yes."

"Stand by, I may need a lift."

"Anywhere," Richard replied expansively. "Husband and son—it would be like Mum losing you and—and Scoop."

"Her only son," Roger pointed out. They were at the back door now and he stepped into the kitchen, rinsed his hands and face at the sink and dried on a towel Richard held out, and went along the passage by the stairs to the front room. It passed momentarily through his mind that it must seem strange to Lady Fellowes, used to luxury, to visit a small suburban house like this, but the thought soon passed.

He heard Janet, his wife, say: "I'm sure I heard Roger."

"You did," Roger said, going into a room furnished comfortably but just as it had been twenty-five years ago. "Hallo, darling." As Janet got up and came towards him, tall and attractive, dark hair only just flecked with grey, he kissed her on the cheek. "Good evening, Lady Fellowes. I am desperately sorry about the attack on your son. There's no worse news, I hope."

Janet showed no surprise, so Lady Fellowes must have talked a little.

"Neither better nor worse about him," Lady Fellowes replied.

"At least, that's hopeful."

"Perhaps," she said. "Perhaps." Richard was right, she was a stunning creature, with that grey hair sweeping down to her shoulders, and her great eyes with their silver grey; and her pallor. "Mr. West, I had to see you urgently."

Janet, bless her, was already out of the room; she closed the door behind her. Roger, trying to reduce the tension which was undoubtedly here, went to the sideboard with its long mirror, and poured himself a whisky and soda; Lady Fellowes's glass, by the chair from which she had risen, was half-full.

"Why?" he asked quietly.

"Helen has been threatened," came the answer, in a hard voice.

Roger held his glass halfway to his mouth, felt his heart thump, and made himself say:

"In the same way as your son?"

"Yes."

"Does she know anything about the blackmail and what caused it?"

"She says she doesn't, but the man who telephoned her said he did not believe a husband would keep such facts from his wife. She's—" Lady Fellowes closed her eyes as she had once that midday, as she went on: "She's been ordered—*ordered*—to leave the country, and told that if she isn't on her way by midnight tonight she will be attacked. Mr. West—" She opened her eyes and their brilliance seemed to dazzle. "Helen wanted to come and see you. *I* want her to leave the country. She cannot help Hubert, but if he recovers only to find her injured—"

"Lady Fellowes," Roger interrupted. "Helen isn't going to be injured. Is she at your apartment?"

"Yes."

"I had a close guard put on it as soon as your son was attacked. While she is there she is in no danger at all." He went to the telephone, an extension of which was in this room, called the Yard and asked for Venables, and ordered: "Have the watch on Lady Fellowes's apartment and the block of flats doubled. If Mrs. Fellowes—Mrs. Hubert Fellowes—goes out, have her both followed and reported on wherever she goes." He rang off on Venables's eager "Right, sir!" and turned to the woman. "The other attacks took us by surprise. It won't happen again."

She asked, levelly: "Is this your way of saying you think Helen should stay in London, Mr. West?"

"It is entirely up to her," answered Roger. "We shall give her all the protection we can if she does stay. I want to talk to her, but I can see her without anyone knowing we've met, if that would help."

"It most certainly would. Mr. West—" Lady Fellowes paused.

"Yes?"

"Do you think you are nearer finding out who is responsible for these crimes?"

"Yes," Roger said. "Your son was attacked by two motor-cyclists. Two motor-cyclists—not necessarily the same two—were caught red-handed this afternoon. One of them was killed. The other is in custody. It is at least conceivable that a gang is involved and these two are members of it."

Those magnificent eyes seemed to glow.

"Captures *already?*"

"These two asked for trouble," Roger said, with a shrug. "We have indications about others. I don't know how soon we shall get results but we've certainly made a start on investigating crimes we didn't know had been committed until this morning. Lady Fellowes, did you come here simply to ask me to protect Helen?"

"Yes," she said quietly. "I really don't feel that I can bear any more, after today. But you have given me a great deal of reassurance. Will you get in touch with my daughter?"

"Yes," Roger promised.

"Then I needn't stay."

"I would like you to stay until I've arranged for protection," Roger said.

"*I* don't need protecting!" She almost laughed, although on a nervous note. "No one would dream that I knew anything about the blackmail. After all, the pressure used against my husband was the threat to tell me."

"You forget one thing," Roger said.

"I don't think so."

"You forget that the blackmailers may think now that I've been to see you, your son might have told you some of the truth; and certainly if they think Helen has any knowledge, she may have confided in you."

"Oh," Lady Fellowes exclaimed, in a low-pitched voice. "I hadn't thought of that. You are quite right, of course." She watched as he went towards the telephone, and when he dialled a number she went on: "You are used to being right, aren't you?" Roger only half-heard her as the Yard operator answered. "Is Mr. Coppell still in his office? . . . Yes, try him . . . Ah! Commander, this is West. I—"

"What's this about you getting your head bashed in?" demanded Coppell, at his gruffest.

"Exaggeration," Roger answered. "I've reason to believe Lady Fellowes may be in grave danger of physical attack and I'd like your confirmation of detailing two men and one woman to watch her closely throughout the emergency."

After a pause, Coppell said: "That's nine officers, in eight hour shifts."

"Yes, sir."

There was another, longer pause before Coppell growled: "I suppose you know what you're doing. All right."

"Will you give the instructions, sir? I'll see her to her home, and after that I'd like to be sure the personal protection is maintained."

"I'll fix it," promised Coppell.

"Thank you, sir."

"What about this youth you killed?" Coppell demanded.

"He fell down the steps and broke his neck. The policeman's action was in simple self-defence," Roger replied.

"I hope the Press agrees."

"Have they been at you, sir?"

"Of course they have. And it won't be long before they're after you. I—well, see me first thing in the morning." Coppell rang off, leaving Roger—as he did so often—with a feeling of disquiet. Sometimes Roger thought it was the nature of the man, at others he thought it was deliberate policy, to keep him on tenterhooks all the time. Schooling himself to show nothing of his feelings, Roger turned to Lady Fellowes, and said:

"That's all done, there's no problem. Would you like to go home now?"

"Yes," she answered promptly.

"I'll come with you," Roger said, "and my son Richard will drive us. Will you have another drink?"

"No, thank you."

"Then I'll just have a word with my wife," Roger said.

Janet and Richard were in the kitchen, and Richard's eyes lit up at the prospect of chauffeuring. Janet seemed to understand and to approve, and dinner, it proved, was a casserole, so it could wait for another hour. She looked rested and sun-bronzed and quite lovely as she hurried along to say goodbye to Lady Fellowes. Richard went out the back way to fetch his car, which he kept in a lean-to attached to the wall of a neighbour's house. Roger used the garage here, which was to one side and a little in front of the house. Its doors were wide open. In five minutes the throb of the engine of his super-charged Mini sounded. Roger took Lady Fellowes out to the car and Janet, who had obviously taken to the other woman.

Richard stood by the open door, in the gathering dusk.

Suddenly, the air seemed to be filled with a different roaring —not the car but a dozen, *dozens* of engines; and as suddenly motor-cyclists turned into the street from each end, and some actually appeared from behind parked cars in Bell Street. One moment it was a quiet, pleasant street with a few houseowners still in their gardens despite the near-darkness; next, the street was filled with the roaring and the reverberating of the motor-cycle engines as the motor-cyclists converged on the scarlet mini. There was no doubt of their aggressive intent.

Richard had no time to get to the wheel.

Roger was by the side of the car, Lady Fellowes bending to get inside.

"Run to the garage!" Roger ordered, close to her ear. "Run for your life!" He raised his voice. "Janet! The garage!" By now three or four of the motor-cyclists were within twenty or thirty yards of them. Every one of the riders wore a crash helmet and

goggles, it was as if visitors from another planet were swarming in Bell Street on their lethal machines.

Richard yelled: "I'll break their necks!"

"Garage!" Roger rasped.

"Garage be damned!" Richard bent double and disappeared into the car and the engine roared, the car started off at shattering speed, heading straight for the nearest motor-cyclists. They swerved, hurling what looked like tennis balls at the car. First the windscreen, then the side window shattered. Other motor-cyclists drew close to Roger's house and hurled missiles at the windows, which crashed in one after another. Janet ran desperately towards the garage where Lady Fellowes already stood. A motor-cyclist jumped the kerb with his front wheel and drew back his right arm to hurl something at her. Roger raised his right leg and kicked the rider off; man and machine went crashing. Richard was halfway along the street, a trail of motor-cycles and riders behind him but others surrounding him, one dragging open a door.

Roger knew it was hopeless, but had to try to help.

Janet, in the garage doorway, was shouting: *"Roger—Roger—Roger!"*

The engines were roaring, the air stank with exhaust fumes, there must be at least forty motor-cyclists still astride their machines. One was leaning inside the mini, obviously trying to pull Richard away from the wheel. Two others raced and roared towards Roger, who would collide with one whichever way he dodged.

As suddenly as the roar of motor-cycle engines, came the wail of a police siren, and a police car swung into the street from King's Road, while another appeared at the other end, but neither blocked the path of the machines. Taken by surprise, the cyclists swerved and instantly some began to ride off towards the corners. Roger, free from danger, ran to the man half in and half out of the mini, and simply bent down, grabbed his ankles

107

and yanked him right out. He came without resistance, banging his chin on the door frame. Roger caught a glimpse of Richard hacking at a man's face with his elbow until the face disappeared.

The sirens wailed, hideously.

Motor-cycle horns began to honk, and engines roared still louder. More police cars turned into the street but could not block it, and a motor-cycle roared off into the night. Roger, deafened, leaned against the car. Richard climbed out on the other side and came round, carrying one of the 'tennis balls' in his hand. It was in fact rather larger, and the way he carried it suggested it was heavy.

"Thanks, Dad," he said. "That was hot while it lasted. But how's this for a clue? These things seem to be made of cement."

13

Breathing Space?

As Richard spoke and Roger took the 'tennis ball' Janet came hurrying, her anxiety written in her eyes and on her face. The last of the motor-cycles had gone but the roar of some engines was still audible. At least one police car was giving chase, while word was going out on walkie-talkies to stop motor-cyclists in the vicinity. Beyond Janet Roger could see at least three motor-cyclists on the ground, with police officers bending over them. There was no way of being sure how many there had been here or how many had escaped.

He took Janet's hands and gripped.

"We're both all right," he said. "Thanks to some miracle."

"Aren't you hurt at all?" she almost screamed.

"I might have a bruise or two," confessed Richard, casually, "but nothing broken. I doubt if Lady Fellowes will want to go in this shattered wagon now," he added, grimacing. "I think I've only one side window whole."

"I'll send her back in a police car," Roger said, slipping an arm round Janet's waist. "I'm all right, really, darling—but I'm not going to be home much tonight."

"*Try* to stay for a meal," pleaded Janet.

By then they were near the house, where Lady Fellowes was bending over a man who had an ugly gash in his cheek; she was stemming the flow of blood with her handkerchief. Police first-aid men came up, two ambulances were on the way, a kind of order was made out of the chaos. More injured motor-cyclists and two passers-by were taken to hospital with the one injured policeman, five motor-cycles—all Hokkis—were collected, and lifted by ropes and loaded into a police van. Newspapermen seemed to have scented the trouble and were already in force—and Roger saw Tweed, the plump man of the *Globe*; his girl photographer was not with him.

By then, Lady Fellowes was on her way back to her apartment in a police car with an escort car, a Chief Inspector was trying to cope with the Press, a garage had sent for Richard's mini and towed it off. Through all of this excitement Roger sat at the kitchen table and ate a casserole with a flavour which only Janet seemed able to give to cooking, which smelt as good as it tasted, while Richard was on the telephone, trying to arrange to borrow a car; Richard never hired if he could borrow; yet contrariwise, he was generous to a fault.

"My!" Roger exclaimed. "That was good, darling, but I couldn't eat any more even if I had nothing to do."

"Whereas you've too much," Janet said. She gave a hard little laugh. "It's quite obvious, but don't worry about me. If it really lasts for night after night I'll go off for a few days."

"Sure you're all right?" Roger insisted.

"Yes." Janet sounded positive, almost as if she had forgotten the days when she had been goaded almost to screaming point because Roger had been kept out night after night. "How long do you think this will last?"

Roger said: "I'd hate to guess."

"It was awful tonight. Like a pitched battle."

"Yes."

"Did you know these motor-cyclists were organized like this?"

"I was beginning to think there was a gang, but had no idea of its strength. I knew of four probable members; now I know there are nearer forty. I suppose there could be four hundred."

"So it's really only the beginning," Janet said.

"Probably," Roger agreed, with forced lightness. "On the

110

other hand this flared up very quickly and could die down as fast." He stood up from the table and went to her, putting his hands on her shoulders and pressing gently. "If you'd really like to go away—"

"Oh, not yet," Janet said, impatiently, looking up at him so that he could see her face upside down. "Darling, please, *please* don't worry about me."

"I won't," promised Roger, and bent down and kissed her forehead.

"Oi-oi-oi!" called Richard, bursting into the kitchen. "How about some of that casserole, Mum, I'm famished! Got a car!" he added, with delight in his voice. "Old Jerry Walker's away for a month, and was going to leave his on the streets, it's not the latest thing in automobiles but it has four wheels and an engine." He washed his hands at the sink, and went on: "Hey, isn't it time we had a letter from Scoop?"

'Scoop', his only brother, older by a year, had emigrated to Australia, and was not the most regular correspondent. Dwelling on him was Richard's way of taking his mother's attention at least partly from what had happened tonight. Ten minutes later, as Roger left the house, Richard actually managed to make her laugh. Roger smiled—and heard a familiar voice as a man said:

"What's so funny, Handsome?"

It was young Tweed, of the *Globe*.

"I'll tell you what isn't funny," Roger said, roughly. "Being called anything but Superintendent by a young cub like you."

Tweed looked taken aback. A man at the rear of a crowd of newspapermen said clearly: "It was time someone tore a strip off that fat lump." Another man called: "What happened, Mr. West? Is it true you were attacked in the city this afternoon?" Yet another called: "What's going on, Superintendent?" And a fourth: "Don't give us the old brush-off, Handsome. This street looked like a battlefield an hour or two ago."

"*And* this fat lump has photographs to prove it." Tweed

raised his voice, so that it was almost shrill; but the way he picked up 'fat lump' and tossed it back did his reputation more good than harm.

Another man called: "Is it true Lady Fellowes was here this evening?"

"I've got a photograph of her, too," called Tweed.

Roger, watching the eager faces of men whom one might have expected to be too blasé to be affected by any sensation, took a quick decision: it might bring Coppell's wrath down on his head, but anything might do that. He would make a statement of a kind. He was aware of his men, watching, and a crowd of neighbours; and of Janet and Richard, drawn somehow from the back of the house. And there was a rumble of voices, as at a cocktail party.

He raised a hand, and the rumbling stopped instantly.

"You know I can't tell you much," he said, "but after tonight's attacks here I will tell you what little I can. Yes, Lady Fellowes was here. There is strong evidence that her husband was being blackmailed, absolutely none that the blackmail had any political significance. There have been a number of other cases of blackmail and attempted blackmail and it is beginning to look as if the blackmail is widespread. It is possible that these motor-cyclists are used to terrify the victims either into paying up or—in some cases—keeping quiet about something they know.

"This afternoon's attack on me, in the city, was undoubtedly directed at me personally. If to prevent me from using knowledge acquired in the investigation, I don't yet know what that knowledge is. Tonight's attack might have been intended for me or Lady Fellowes. You know that her son was attacked at midday by two motor-cyclists, presumably because he was believed to know more than anyone else about the blackmail of his father. His wife and his mother have both assured me that they know absolutely nothing." He paused, and repeated in a clear voice: "I regard this as a matter of extreme importance. Both his wife, Helen Fellowes, and his mother, Lady Fellowes, have assured me that they know absolutely nothing—that Hubert Fellowes did not confide in them. If you quote me on that, make sure it's verbatim, please."

Several of the newspapermen were scribbling. He waited for them to finish before going on:

"One last thing: Professor Clayton who was brutally attacked at his Hampstead home by two motor-cyclists was also being blackmailed, and his assailants were believed to be riding Japanese-made Hokki machines like those used in Bell Street tonight." He paused again, raised both hands and said: "That's the lot!" and strode forward. They cleared a path for him and there at the end of the path was Jones, his car behind him.

"Thanks," Roger said, and climbed in.

Questions were called, but he distinguished none and no one was particularly insistent. A uniformed policeman cleared away a crowd, neighbours and passers-by, and as the car drove off there was a ragged cheer. Roger sat back and closed his eyes, and without opening them, asked:

"Who sent the cars, Jones?"

"I think it was Sergeant Venables," Jones answered.

"Ah," breathed Roger. "What brought you back?"

"I picked up *Information's* call for all cars in the vicinity to rush to Bell Street, so I knew you were in trouble. Very glad it wasn't worse, sir."

"Thanks."

"And we've caught five—enough of the baskets to make some of them talk, surely."

"We'll see," Roger said.

He was at the new building within fifteen minutes; the move to Victoria Street and Broadway had been an advantage to him, saving at least fifteen minutes' driving. He went in without being noticed and up to the fourth floor, carrying three of the cement spheres, and turned into Venables's office and found the sergeant leaning back in his chair, a sandwich in one hand, the telephone in the other.

"Sorry, Mum," he was saying, "but I don't think I'll make it. Don't wait up." He caught sight of Roger and was suddenly a surge of motion, gasped: "Goodbye!" banged the receiver down and missed the platform, gulped down his mouthful of sandwich and gave a despairing look at the wastepaper basket.

"Now take it easy," Roger urged, squatting on the corner of his desk. "What made you send out an alarm call for Bell Street?"

Venables gave a final gulp, and stood up—and banged his head on a picture just behind him.

"I—er—I—er—I heard Lady Fellowes had gone to your place, sir, and I checked with Division and they said there were a lot of motor-cycles about. I didn't want to trouble you so I—er—what I did *was* all right, wasn't it?" he burst out.

"Perfectly. What did Division actually say?"

"Well, they said a Hokki Motor-Cycle Club seemed to be meeting on the Embankment near you. I thought it wouldn't do any harm if we had a concentration of cars. Are *you* all right, sir?"

"Thanks to you. I'm alive, thanks to you," Roger said. "So is my son. So is Lady Fellowes."

Venables gave a broad, happy smile—and then began to cough, apparently on a crumb in his throat. Roger gripped his shoulder tightly and then went into his own office. He sat very still for a long time; reaction was catching up with him. It was some minutes before he pulled a file towards him, opened it, and saw a brief report headed *Battle of Bell Street*. There were times when Venables, for all his ungainliness and his nervousness, could act with the speed of light.

The report read:

An attack appears to have been made by a colony of motor-cy-clists, estimated at between forty and fifty, on Chief Superintend-ent Roger West and also apparently on Lady Diana Fellowes in Bell Street, Chelsea, at approximately 6.45 this evening.

Five of the motor-cyclists were injured in a conflict with police and with Mr. West and his son Richard. All five are in the St. Stephen's Hospital. Three of the motor-cyclists were arrested in Bell Street and charged with committing a breach of the peace, and seven motor-cyclists have since been held, pending charges. As these seven were not caught in Bell Street there is not yet sufficient evidence of their involvement.

None of the men detained has yet made any statement. All are members of a club known as the London Central Hokki Motor Cycle Braves, one of many Hokki clubs in the country. All those arrested, according to medical reports, are 'on' drugs, probably heroin.

The motor-cycles used were in all cases Japanese Hokki machines, Mark III of medium weight and 500 c.c. engines. The owners (or mechanics used by them) bore out the cylinders to 600 c.c. and add larger carburettors and jets, for extra power. All use rear wheel drag slicks (i.e. have smooth rear tyres, which screech on the road, and straight exhaust pipes, which cause more noise). All the machines examined have fibre glass fenders and petrol tanks for lessening weight and so increasing speed and acceleration.

Each of the motor-cyclists carried a net bag which contained a number of cement balls, about the size of a tennis ball, as aggressive weapons. Many of these were thrown.

A list of names, registration numbers and addresses was attached to this report.

Roger read this through again, and listened for coughing, heard none, and rang for Venables, who came in promptly. He had wiped away all traces of crumbs and tears, his colour was normal, and he took extreme care not to bang against the door or desk.

"You rang, sir."

"Yes," Roger said, and motioned to an upright chair with a padded back. "Sit down."

"Thank you, sir." Venables sat with care, easing his trousers about his knees. There was something boyish about him, and appealing. Roger had first come to know him when he had been assigned to a gold bullion case. Venables had proved to be a dedicated policeman, with two defects. First: his clumsiness and, at that time particularly, his lack of self-confidence. Second: he was nauseated by the odour of decaying flesh, and for a policeman who might be involved in a murder investigation at any time, this was a serious drawback. To help overcome it, he had spent some weeks in the pathological laboratory with one of the leading Home Office pathologists, who had afterwards telephoned Roger.

"He'll always be squeamish but he won't flop out again. He's beaten the worst of the problem."

"Venables," Roger said quietly, "I was absolutely serious in your office. I owe you my life—they would have killed me. I don't think Richard would have survived, either."

"I can only say I'm very, *very* glad," Venables replied. "It was the word from Chelsea Division about a club meeting which really alerted me. May I ask a question, sir?"

"Go ahead."

"Why do you think these people want you dead?"

"I might have come across some information they don't want me to pass on," Roger said, as he had told the newspapermen. "If I have I don't yet know what it is. Have you any ideas?"

"No," answered Venables. "But I've been through all the notes you gave me and made a note of all the information you've mentioned in passing. If I put it all in a detailed report, will you go through it and correct anything that's wrong and put in anything I've omitted? That way," Venables went on earnestly, "we may find out the motive for the attacks on you. Until we do, you'll be in very grave danger. You ought to have a bodyguard wherever you go. You do realise that, don't you, sir?" he finished, and his tone and his expression were alike, pleading; he was like a great bloodhound, asking for a reward for following a scent.

14

Grave Danger?

Roger looked into Venables's big, rather doe-like eyes, and said gruffly: "It's damned hard to believe." But in fact it was almost certainly true. It was next door to inconceivable that a campaign should suddenly be launched against a senior officer of the Yard, but Venables believed it; and so did he.

Other facts passed through his mind.

He had been back from Southern Africa for two days; only two days. For most of the first he had sat twiddling his thumbs in this office. So in twenty-four hours the blackmailers had gone into action like a well-trained army corps. At first it had seemed improbable that they should have two members close enough to attack Hubert Fellowes; it had seemed just as unlikely that two could be stationed close enough to attack him in the quiet street leading to Old Jewry.

"Estimated at between forty and fifty," he observed.

"All the reports say that, sir."

"All on Hokki motor-cycles?"

"And all wearing heavy goggles large enough to disguise all the face except the mouth and chin," Venables put in.

"Clothes?"

"Brown plastic imitation leather jackets with the collars turned up."

"Hiding the mouth and chin," Roger remarked.

"In many cases, yes, sir. And a kind of jeans."

"Kind of?" asked Roger.

"Either blue jeans or grey jeans with the usual pockets, low-cut waistlines and contour fit."

"You know," said Roger, "we want a complete outfit for close examination and we want to find out where they are made."

"*Very* good idea, sir!"

"We also want to find out where these are manufactured," Roger went on, touching one of the concrete balls. It would be easy enough with wooden or cast iron or plastic moulds."

"Anywhere they make balls of that size for children," Venables hazarded.

"Right! Toy makers."

"So we need a list of toy makers who might have moulds of that size," Roger said. "And we want to find out if any of them have lost a mould or two recently." He paused, looking intently at Venables. "What's the name of the club these men are believed to belong to?"

"Known to belong to, sir—they had membership cards and the Hokki badge, an H in Japanese-type lettering. The London Central Hokki Motor-Cycle Braves," finished Venables, "and—" He broke off.

"Go on."

"There are at least four other branches."

"Where?"

"South West London, North London, South East and East— you might say sou'south east, sir."

Roger said, softly: "Do the Divisions know all these?"

"Yes—and probably more."

Roger picked up the cement ball, and tossed it a few inches into the air. Even as he caught it the impact was enough to sting. Hurled into a man's face, or head, it could kill; if it was hurled against any part of the body it could break bones and cause a serious injury.

"I may be locking the stable door after the horse has bolted, but we want all of these clubs raided—tonight."

118

Venables gulped. "Sir," he muttered.

"You haven't had them raided!" exclaimed Roger.

"No, sir, oh no, I wouldn't do that without authority, but I have asked all Divisions to keep a close watch, and to question any members who leave the various club headquarters. So they're all set to raid, sir—I think it would be a jolly good idea."

Jolly good idea, Roger thought—it was like listening to Richard, years ago. He was still deliberating when he heard heavy footsteps in the passage; at any other time he would have thought: Coppell. The door burst open and Coppell strode in, massive in white tie and tails which fitted and suited him perfectly.

Roger stood up; Venables seemed glued to his chair.

"Good evening—" began Roger.

"They told me you were dead!" roared Coppell.

"A near miss, sir," Roger replied, and then motioned to Venables, who had at last reached his feet but looked as if he were about to collapse. "But only just. If Detective Sergeant Venables had not moved with exceptional speed and anticipation I think I would be dead."

Coppell turned to Venables, who forced himself to stand to attention.

"I—ah. I only—ah—did the obvious thing, sir," he stammered.

"It wouldn't have been obvious to many people," Roger remarked drily.

"Hmmph," grunted Coppell. "Well, as you're still in the land of the living you can tell me all about this." His gaze roamed and he caught sight of the heading of Venables's report and read it quite literally—"*Battle of Bell Street*. How many of the little bastards did we catch?"

Roger paused.

"F-five hurt, three charged and seven held," Venables blurted.

"Talked to them yet?" Coppell made this question direct to Roger.

"No," Roger answered, "and I'd rather try to pick up some

119

more before starting to question them. There are some motor-cycle clubs . . ." He explained briefly, with Coppell nodding after every sentence or so, and finished: "The Divisions are watching the club houses, and—" He paused, for Venables made a sound like 'kkk' as if he wanted to interrupt, but he thought better of it, and Roger went on: "I'd like to raid them, tonight."

Coppell was still Coppell.

"All by yourself?" he demanded.

"I thought the Divisions might help, and we might use the Flying Squad from here, leaving a skeleton staff for emergency."

"Do that," Coppell approved, beginning to turn on his heel. "If you get any results which can't wait until morning, send a message to me at the Mansion House—Lord Mayor's Charity Banquet."

"I will, sir."

Coppell strode out, turned back with surprising agility for so big a man, and seemed to glower at Venables. And to Roger's astonishment, he said:

"None of us want to lose West. Look after him, Sergeant."

He was out of the office with the door swinging behind him before Venables began to turn from grey to white, white to pink, pink to purple. Roger sat as his desk and opened a file, and for the first time saw a diagram which Venables had drawn, showing the Metropolitan Police area in outline, and also showing the four places where the Hokki Motor-Cycle Braves had clubs. One was in Fulham; one in Camberwell, one near Charlton, and the fourth in Tottenham. He glanced at Venables, and said:

"Go to your office and tell Fulham I hope to be there in half-an-hour. Meanwhile will they make all preparations for a raid and then tell Camberwell to make a raid—I'll be there an hour later. You take the Divisions which cover Charlton and Tottenham—better do Tottenham first and Charlton immediately after, and you get to the second one as soon as you can. All clear?"

"Absolutely, sir!"

"Tell all Divisions they'll have Flying Squad assistance, tell them to let none of the Braves leave until you or I have been there. I'll give you a note of authority before you go. I'll talk to *Information* and the Flying Squad. Get a move on, don't stand gawping!"

Venables went out of the room like a frightened rabbit.

Roger was smiling as he picked up the telephone.

Forty minutes later, he was at the headquarters of the South West Division, talking to a Chief Inspector in charge. The club known as the Hokki Motor-Cycle Braves was one of at least a dozen groups or clubs in the area. It—like the others—organised rallies, races, hill trials, cross country runs. This particular club was well known because several of its members had been pulled in for pushing drugs, mostly L.S.D., but there was no evidence that all the members bought or were addicts. The Hokki Braves were mostly small youths and men, for the Hokki motor-cycle was the smallest of the standard machines but with a powerful 500 c.c. engine. This could be supercharged until the machine had remarkable acceleration, as well as top speeds of well over one hundred and fifty miles on the open road.

"Do they behave themselves?" asked Roger.

"Now and again we pull one in for speeding," said Hill, the man in charge. He was a tall, lean man with an almost completely bald head. "Their camp—"

"Camp?"

"They call it a camp, not a club," said Hill, drily. "It's on the Eelbrook Common. Do you know it?"

"I live in Chelsea," Roger reminded him.

"Oh, yes. Well, they're demolishing some houses facing the common and the Braves rent two or three of them—the last to be demolished—and use the houses as camp headquarters. They have plenty of parking space on the edge of the common and on the empty demolition sites."

"How many are there now?" asked Roger.

"I've had the place under surveillance since the Battle of Bell Street," Hill replied. "A few members have gone in, only one has come out and we held him for questioning. He hasn't said a word yet."

Roger had an uneasy feeling that the man would not talk.

"Let's close in," he said.

"Expect any resistance?" asked Hill.

"They might use iron piping, bicycle chains or these," said Roger, holding out the cement ball. "Do you have riot shields here?"

"Yes."

"Better have them handy," Roger said.

Fifteen minutes after he had arrived, he went with Hill in a car to the nearest spot to the houses which were used by the Hokki Braves. Light shone at the windows, and music from radio or a record player came clearly over the night air. Six or seven motor-cycles stood on their rests, just outside. Roger, knowing it would be easy to make it look as if he wanted to hog all the limelight, stayed near while Hill and two of his men approached the front door. With Flying Squad men at least thirty police officers encircled the two small houses, once part of a long terrace at the Fulham Broadway end of the triangular-shaped common.

Hill banged on the door; there was no reply.

He banged again and called clearly: "Open, in the name of the law!"

There was still no reply, and Hill stood aside, ordering his men: "Break it down."

The flimsy front door fell in on the third assault. Light streamed out, showing the branches of trees on the common, and the sound of music became much louder. Hill went in first, with his men close behind and others, including Roger, close on their heels.

The only sounds were the music and the thump of footsteps.

No one was in the house, but the seven records on a record player indicated the men had been here only a short while ago.

"They must have had scouts out, seen us, and sneaked off without their motor-cycles," Hill said, bitterly. "My chaps were waiting to hear the cycles. Mr. West, I feel dreadful about this. Feel I've fallen right down on the job."

"I've a nasty feeling all the others will have been fooled, too," Roger said, glumly. "You shouldn't blame yourself too much."

"I do, all the same," Hill said.

"Let's have a look at the motor-cycles," Roger said. "If they're the same as were used in Bell Street, the engines have been hotted up, and they're tuned and doctored for speed and noise."

"We'll soon see," said Hill.

The first machine, standing on its rest near the back door, had full tread on the rear tyre. Nothing indicated that it had been supercharged. A Flying Squad man spent five minutes taking the engine down, and announced:

"No one's bored this one out, sir."

None of the machines here was a 'special'. Roger went inside where Hill and two of his men were searching for any sign of drugs. There was coffee, tea, milk, sugar, biscuits, nuts, even the ingredients for hot dogs and hamburgers as well as a variety of tinned food; but there were no drugs and no indication that any had ever been used.

"They couldn't have cleaned the place up so thoroughly," Hill argued. "If some of them are users and others pushers, they don't operate here."

"Doesn't look like it," Roger agreed. "I wonder what there'll be at the other places."

As they were heading for the Camberwell 'camp' word came through from there and also from Tottenham that the raids at each place had been abortive—obviously the Hokki Braves had anticipated them, and got away before the raid. The same proved true of the camp in Charlton. No drugs were found; no cement missiles, no supercharged motor-cycles.

"They expected to be raided and they just cleared out," Venables said, miserably. "I ought to have ordered the raids earlier, sir."

"You stuck your neck out quite far enough," Roger said. "They may have disappeared but they haven't vanished from the face of the earth. And they may have a hide-out we haven't discovered yet. Moreover all the Braves may not be involved. Go home, get a good night's sleep, and come in before nine in the morning. We've a heavy day in front of us."

"Sir?" ventured Venables.

"Yes?"

"Shouldn't we send out word for reports on all motor-cycles seen in the streets tonight?"

"It wouldn't do any harm," Roger conceded, "but I think we'll find that these chaps have gone to ground for a day or two. They'll probably wait for our next move before they make theirs."

"*I* think you're still in very grave danger, sir," Venables insisted. "I really don't think you ought to go home or anywhere without an escort."

Roger looked at him very steadily.

He was probably right; but seldom in his career had he been so scared that he had wanted protection. He did not want it now, everything in him reacted against it. Once he allowed himself to be forced into such a defensive position, once he admitted that it was not safe to walk about or drive alone, it would be a major concession to the other side, and that could not only improve their morale enormously, but it could weaken his—and, although they might not realise it, could affect many men at the Yard.

Slowly, he shook his head.

"Not yet," he said. "The time might come, but not yet." He

dismissed the subject by squaring his shoulders and exclaiming: "Now! The Divisions will be getting all the information they can on these so-called camps. And first thing in the morning we want to start tracing all Hokki owners through the licensing departments in the various boroughs. We'll charge them with breach of the peace then let all the prisoners stew for the night, I think. Before I go home, though, I want to check on Professor Clayton and Hubert Fellowes."

Clayton was reported to be 'a little better'.

Young Fellowes was still in the intensive care unit; the operation for brain damage was successful as far as the surgeons could judge, but there was an ever present danger of a relapse.

All was quiet at the flat where Lady Fellowes and Helen were still together.

"So Helen didn't go," Roger mused aloud. "I thought it would take a lot to make her. I—but sergeant!"

Venables started up. "Sir?"

"Young Kevin Spray! I'd forgotten him. Where is he?"

"He's in the waiting room here, sir," said Venables, and added guiltily: "I didn't have time to mention him in my report. There's a note about his mother, too. She telephoned twice this afternoon, wanting to know if there was any news of him. I didn't tell her, of course."

"I'll go down and see him right away," Roger said.

"Do you really think you should, sir?" asked Venables, in one of his curiously daring moods. "Wouldn't it be better to leave them *all* until the morning? All the Hokki Braves, I mean."

There was a long silence before Roger asked heavily: "Is Kevin Spray a Hokki Brave?"

"Oh yes, sir," answered Venables. "That's a thing I learned too late to put in my report. There's a Hokki Braves camp in a lot of universities, including London. I sent a general request out to the police in all university cities for information and a great deal of it's in. This organisation isn't restricted to London, sir. It's nationwide."

15

Kevin Spray

Roger went down to the waiting room by himself, still shaken by what Venables had told him. Was the sergeant right? Was the organisation which had leapt to action so quickly really nationwide? Were all clubs which called themselves the Hokki Motor-Cycle Braves involved in crimes of violence?

"I simply don't believe it," Roger said aloud as he walked along a passage very similar to the one on his floor.

At the old Yard, prisoners had been kept handy at Cannon Row, the police station which was close by; there was no such facility in the new new Scotland Yard, but some rooms on this floor had reinforced doors and windows, and two had reverse windows; one could see in from outside but not out from inside. The two rooms were virtually cells, and anyone under charge and particularly anyone who might become violent, was invariably kept in one of them. Kevin Spray was in the first.

A policeman in uniform was just outside the door.

"How is he?" asked Roger.

"Asleep, as a matter of fact, sir. He got into a bit of a paddy an hour ago but after a bit of dinner he settled down and dropped off." The constable unlocked the door and Roger went into the small but comfortable waiting room. A plainclothes man sat in one corner armchair, newspaper by his side, a paperback book on his knees. Kevin Spray lay at full length on a couch which was amply long enough for him. His shoes were

126

placed neatly by the side of the couch, and his brown leather or plastic leather jacket was folded over another armchair. He wore a well-washed pair of jeans: the Hokki Braves' uniform.

The plainclothes man, in middle years and corpulent, got to his feet.

"Shall I wake him, sir?"

"Leave him to me," Roger said. "You take a breather."

"Thank you, sir."

"Tell the man outside to watch, in case I need some help."

"Not much fear of that, Mr. West—but I'll tell him." The man went out.

Kevin Spray showed no sign that he had been disturbed. He lay on his right side, facing the room, one arm over the top of his face, obviously to shade his eyes from the light. He breathed deeply and evenly. Roger moved close to him, vividly reminded of his own sons when they had been younger. He could not really see the youth's face but the chin and mouth were very like Ida Spray's. Gently, Roger began to move the protecting arm, then shifted his position so that his head cast a shadow over the top of the other's head. Next he finished lowering the arm, so that it rested, still bent, on the flat stomach.

Roger studied the young face.

Kevin Spray, being fair, did not look as if he needed to shave regularly; 'boyish' was undoubtedly the word for him. But his forehead, jutting eyebrows and deepset eyes as well as his aquiline nose were unmistakably his father's. It was seldom that both parents were so clearly reflected in a face.

Boyish, Roger thought; and innocent. This was the deep, untroubled sleep of youth.

"Kevin," Roger said, in a clear voice, but it had no effect. "Kevin!" He raised his voice, and the youth began to stir. He placed a hand on the other's shoulder and gripped firmly. "Kevin—wake up."

The stirring stopped, and he knew that the other was awake, and wary, but not watchful; after a momentary flicker, his eyelids did not move. In a quieter, less authoritative voice, Roger spoke again.

"Kevin, I am Chief Superintendent West, and I have a message from your mother."

The youth's eyes opened. They were a vivid blue, and very large. He did not move a muscle of his body, but stared intently at Roger, who sensed he was going to have problems; there was a stubborn set to Kevin Spray's jaw and hardness in those blue eyes.

"I don't want to hear it," he said in a flat voice.

"She is worried out of her mind."

"If she'd worried more about me before she wouldn't be worrying so much now." The bitterness seemed unmistakable, and the boy's emotions appeared to be as much disturbed because of his mother as his father.

Roger said: "Sometimes young people of student age can be the most cruel, callous and ignorant of all human beings. Are you?"

"I hate her for what she's done to me, the lying bitch."

Roger felt a mixture of compassion and disgust for this young man. It was understandable if not pleasant that he should over-react against his mother. He waited a few moments under the defiant stare of those blue eyes, and then said almost casually:

"And you hate your father so much that you smashed his head in. If he dies, you'll get imprisonment for life. Do you realise that?"

At last Kevin moved; his whole body took on a convulsive movement as he sprang up, and swung his legs off the couch; anger and perhaps fear now drove the defiance from his eyes.

"What the hell do you mean?"

"You know what I mean."

"I didn't attack my father! All I wanted was to get to hell away from the whole bloody situation."

Roger began to frown; and slowly opened the *Evening News*

which had the story of the attack on Professor Clayton on the front page, as well as a picture of Clayton and his wife.

"You own a Hokki motor-cycle," Roger said accusingly.

"Why shouldn't I?"

"You were riding about north-west London last night."

"So what?"

"Soon after the attack on your father—"

"Stop calling him my father!" cried Kevin, in sudden fury. "He's never acknowledged me, he's pretended to be *Uncle* Oliver. I don't want to hear of him again—or of her. I just want to blot them out of my mind."

"Soon after the attack on your father—"

Kevin struck out at him, and at the same time shifted to one side of the couch and tried to spring to his feet. Roger grabbed his wrist, blocked the punch, twisted and sent the youth thudding back onto the couch; the breath seemed to be driven out of his body and he sat glaring.

"You're not dealing with a defenceless man now," Roger rasped.

"I—I didn't attack anyone."

"You rode through the night to Harwich and tried to catch the morning ferry."

"I tell you all I wanted was to get away from England. My God, how I hate the hypocritical stinking people! How—"

"Like millions of others you've lived here nearly twenty years, haven't done a stroke of work, have been fed, given money, educated for nothing—is that why the English people stink? If you go abroad you'll have the protection of a British passport, and—"

"To hell with you!"

"Kevin," Roger said in a quieter voice, "why did you attack your father?"

"I didn't attack him! It's a damned lie!"

"Is it?" asked Roger, insistently. "What happened the day before yesterday to make you try to run away?"

"I've every right to go where I want to! I'll—" Kevin began to look about him as if desperately; as if he felt cornered. Roger moved his chair back, and the youth sprang to his feet and began to pace up and down. "I just wanted to get away, anywhere out of England, out of sight and sound of my mother. All these years she's lied to me! Uncle Oliver, Uncle Oliver, kind uncle, thank you uncle, he's very kind to you. Uncle! Kind! He's my father and hadn't the guts to admit it! He kept mother stuffed away in a little apartment while he lived in luxury with his wife and *real* children. The swine! The bloody lecher!"

His voice was rising. He was clenching his hands and swinging his arms by his sides as he moved about. Now and again he looked at Roger; most of the time he glared at the ceiling as if invoking the heavens.

"If they'd told me when I was a kid it wouldn't have mattered. It's living a lie I hate. My mother lived a lie, so did he, and they made me live one, too. My God, how I hate them!"

"Enough to try to kill," said Roger flatly.

Kevin swung round and screamed: "No! No, no, no, no, a thousand times bloody no. I didn't attack him. He wouldn't be worth a lifetime in prison!"

"Two youths on motor-cycles attacked him savagely."

"Do I *look* like two?" screeched Kevin.

"You and your friend Higginbottom who can't be traced, make two," Roger retorted.

"Higginbottom?" Kevin was shaken.

"Yes. Did you tell him that you'd discovered who your father was?"

"Did I tell him? Good God, no! *He told me*! He saw the two of us together a few weeks ago, and saw the likeness. That was when I first began to realise the truth. I hadn't before, but—well, Higgy got a photograph of *him* from a newspaper and placed it next to one of mine. There couldn't be any doubt. I didn't want to believe it, but I had to know. So—so I confronted mother and—my God! She admitted it. The whore, she—"

"Don't call her bitch or whore again in my hearing," Roger said coldly.

"That's what she is!"

"She is the woman who bore you, nurtured you, looked after you, lived for you," Roger said. "One day, if you ever grow up, you'll know just how much doing all that cost her. Did you go to Hampstead—your father's house—the day before yesterday?"

Kevin cried: "Yes, but I didn't attack him!"

"When did you go?"

"I was going to make him see me, I was going to force my way in and confront him and his wife! I just wanted to see him suffer, I didn't care what I had to do to make him. Can't you understand *that*?"

"I can understand without liking it but what I like is neither here nor there," Roger said. "Did you force your way in?"

"No!"

"Why not?"

"I—I found out that I couldn't when it came to the point. I walked up and down outside the house, and—oh, hell! I saw his wife come in. I *saw* her. She—well, there was something about her. I don't know what, but there was something. I just felt—well I realised *she* was a victim just as much as I. He'd lived a lie with her for over twenty years; when she found out the truth she would feel like hell. And—and somehow I couldn't make myself go in. I couldn't be the one who told her the truth. I just couldn't do it."

Kevin stopped, squarely in front of Roger. There was a different expression in his eyes, a mixture of bewilderment and anger. He stood as if ready to attack yet made no movement; it was as if something had struck him until he could neither move nor speak.

Gradually, words formed at the back of his throat; hoarse, harsh.

"I could not do it. I could not make her suffer. That—that is

131

really why I ran away. I couldn't face—face—I couldn't face my mother or *him* or—or even myself. I had to run away."

Roger asked, quietly: "From yourself?"

"From everything I was. Everything I'd made myself. Everything I remember. All the lies and all the cheating."

"Not your lies and not your cheating," Roger reminded him.

"You don't think so?" The young voice was still harsh but not so effortful. "That shows how much *you* know about human nature. I'd told everyone he was my uncle. That my father had died in Australia before she came to England. That she had inherited enough money from him to keep her going. But what was the truth? She was a kept woman. Her part-time job is a fake. My God, how much worse can it be? How much lower can you get than a purveyor of secondhand lies?"

He turned away at last, and Roger thought he was going to rush to the door to try to escape. But he did not. He looked round again and went on scathingly: "And you had to bring me back. You had to send right across England and bring me back. I suppose the next thing you try will be to sick my mother onto me."

For a few minutes while those words had come with their mood of utter despair, Roger had felt sorry for the youth; a deep compassion. Now Spray had caused a complete revulsion of feeling. Roger knew that his own mood was vacillating; that he was tired and suffering from reaction; he could not really rely on his judgment. But he could not prevent another wave of disgust. Obviously it was revealed in his expression, for the youth stood still again, staring; it was as if what he saw was hurtful.

"No," Roger made himself say. "I'm not going to let you meet your mother tonight—and incidentally her job is as real as your father's. You haven't been charged yet, but the fact that you were at Hampstead and blood was found on your motor-cycle, while tracks of its tyres were identified at the house in Beacon Road, justifies us making a charge." He paused, but the other made no comment. "If you're charged you'll spend the night in a police station cell."

"What are you going to charge me with?"

"Don't act like an oaf," Roger said roughly. "I'll charge you with causing Professor Clayton grievous bodily harm and have you held in custody for a week if you don't change your tune. How long have you been a Hokki Brave?"

"A Hokki— Oh, *that* group! About a year."

"Has Higginbottom been in the same time?"

"A few months longer," Kevin said.

"Do you bore out your cylinders and hot the machine up?"

"Do *I*? No—I'm satisfied with my 500 c.c., I—"

"Does Higginbottom hot *his* up?"

Kevin gulped. "I—I don't know."

"You know. Does he hot his machine up?" When Kevin didn't answer Roger went on: "You really want a week in the cells, don't you?"

"He—he does, sometimes."

"Does he use a smooth rear tyre?"

"I—sometimes, he likes the noise it makes."

"He likes to scare the wits out of people in the streets," Roger rasped. "Is he a pusher?"

"A *what?*"

"Take that innocent look off your face. You know what a pusher is."

"You—you mean, drugs?"

"I mean heroin and the hard stuff."

"I don't know!" cried Kevin. "He's never tried to make me take them. I don't think he is, but I can't be sure." The youth moistened his lips. "What are you driving at? The Hokki Braves are just members of a club—"

"Some of them are killers, some of them are pushers and some of them are drug users," Roger said. "Don't pretend you didn't know."

"But—but I didn't know!" protested Kevin Spray hoarsely. "I swear I didn't!"

It was impossible to be sure that he was telling the truth, but he stuck to his denial under ten minutes of vigorous questioning. He *thought* some of the Braves were drug users but no drug had ever been pushed to him, and he was sure that most of them were Braves simply because of the exhilaration of belonging to an unusual club.

"There's no way I can prove what I say," he muttered.

"You'd better try to convince me," Roger said.

"What difference will it make?" muttered Kevin.

"This difference. If you give me your assurance that you will come here to see me at ten o'clock in the morning, you can leave and spend the night wherever you want to. I'll need ten minutes to complete a few formalities, that's all."

As he spoke, the youth's eyes glowed as they had not done that night. When Roger had finished, the other looked almost radiant as he breathed:

"You believe me?"

"I think there's a fifty-fifty chance that you're telling the truth."

"I *am* telling the truth, I swear it," Kevin Spray declared with great earnestness. "And yes—I'll be here at ten o'clock in the morning. I swear that, too!"

"Good," Roger said. "I'll be back in a few minutes."

In fact, moving as fast as he knew how, it took him seven to make sure that Kevin Spray would be followed wherever he went; and that every policeman on duty in London that night had his description and all police at airports and railway stations were warned to look out for him. Then he went back to the waiting room, where the youth had his shoes and jacket on, ready to leave. Roger escorted him to the main doors, and offered him a police car.

"No, I'll walk for ten minutes, then get a cab," Kevin said. Two taxis with lighted signs showing they were vacant passed,

134

heading in the Victoria direction as they reached the doors which opened onto Victoria Street. Roger expected the youth to rush away but Kevin hesitated, as if there was something on his mind. In the light of the street lamps his face was shadowed; and he looked much more like his father than his mother.

Suddenly, he blurted out: "How is he? How is—I mean, how is Professor Clayton? He's not dead, is he?"

The very tone and expression seemed to merge together in a great pleading that the answer should be: "No, your father is alive."

16

The Hokki Clubs

"No," Roger said. "He isn't dead. He's still in a very bad way, the attack was so savage, but the last I heard there was good hope that he would pull through."

"Thanks," Kevin muttered. "Thanks very much." He turned and ran down the steps, then turned left, towards Westminster Abbey and the Houses of Parliament. He walked at great speed, obviously in good physical condition. Roger watched him for half-a-minute, by which time he was practically out of sight. Very few people were about; very few cars. He turned, heard the sonorous chimes of Big Ben, and glanced at his watch.

It was one o'clock.

"I don't want many more days like this," he said aloud, and went inside, stifling a yawn. He was tempted to have another word with Venables, decided against it, and walked from the Victoria Street entrance to the Broadway one, where there were signs of life. Two or three youngish detective officers were in a corner, laughing; the man on desk duty looked across at them as if in warning.

"Goodnight, sir."

"Is someone outside with a car?" asked Roger.

"Oh yes, sir. Sergeant!" The desk duty man raised his voice to a parade ground voice, and the three men stopped laughing, and turned. "One of you drive Mr. West home—it *is* home you want, isn't it, sir?"

"Just as soon as I can get there," Roger answered.

One of the detectives, shorter and plumper than the other two, came hurrying. "I will, sir!" In another corner two plainclothes men were talking to a little woman who seemed about to burst into tears. A uniformed man and a long-haired youth in a shiny brown jacket and jeans came in through one set of swing doors as Roger went out of the other. "One of these Hokki Braves," the plump sergeant observed, opening the back of the car standing outside.

"I'll sit in the front," Roger said.

"Right, sir." A door slammed, another opened. The plump young officer moved with startling speed and was soon turning into Victoria Street.

"What do you know of the Hokki Braves?" asked Roger.

"I've seen 'em about for some months," said the sergeant. "One of my kid brothers is crazy to get a Hokki and join them."

"Oh," Roger said. "How old is he?"

"Fourteen, sir."

"He'll have a couple of years to wait yet for his licence. They're pretty strong, aren't they?"

"Very numerous, sir," the sergeant said. "But I didn't expect anything like tonight's affair. Proper battle, wasn't it?"

"Yes."

"*Very* glad you weren't hurt, sir."

"Thanks," Roger said, and went on in the same breath: "Have you seen many about tonight?"

"Hokki Braves, sir—no, very few."

"Do you know if every Hokki owner is a Brave?"

"I don't, sir, but I've a feeling it's a very well organised group. They—I mean the Hokki distributors in England—do a very good public relations job, and there are a lot of advantages in being a Brave." There was no doubt, he used 'Brave' in exactly the same tone as he would 'a club member'. "Spare parts are all at wholesale prices, there are easy-to-win competitions, food is cheap and so are the outfits they wear at the camps."

137

"Beer?" asked Roger.

"Oh, no beer, sir—no alcohol at all."

"That's something," Roger said. He nearly asked 'drugs' but stopped himself. If this man had any suspicion that the Hokki Braves were used to distribute drugs, he would have said so. It was surprising how much he had learned from what was a chance acquaintance; though Venables would no doubt soon come up with this. It was equally surprising how many Hokkis there were in London.

Soon, they turned into Bell Street. Two policemen were at the King's Road end and Roger was sure he saw others; clearly the local division and the Yard were taking no chances. The sergeant asked:

"Which house, sir?"

"Past the third lamp-post on the left—the one with the garage that juts out a bit. What's your name, by the way?"

"Bird, sir, Detective Sergeant Bird, I've just been assigned to the Flying Squad. Er—that was my father at the desk tonight. He's been in the Force for thirty years."

"Runs in the family, eh?"

"*My* son will carry on with the tradition or *I'll* know the reason why! My grandfather was in the Force, too, sir."

"Well, well," Roger said. "That really is a police family. Goodnight."

"Goodnight, sir."

Roger was smiling faintly to himself. He could understand the elderly man at the desk being concerned about the trio's hilarity; and sensed, moreover, a deep pride in membership of the Metropolitan Police. How many men were three-rising-four generations old in the Force? he wondered.

The main bedroom light was out. There was a low wattage lamp burning in the hall, another in the kitchen, a third on the landing. In the kitchen there was soup in a saucepan, ready to warm, and sandwiches in a plastic wrap beneath a basin. Sandwiches under a basin to keep them moist was another

138

tradition! Instant coffee was already in a cup, there was the right amount of water to heat quickly in the kettle. He was too tired, really, but he had two sandwiches and some milk, then went quietly upstairs.

Janet had left the bedroom door open.

These days, they slept in twin beds, hers near the window so that if he were called out during the night, or came in late like this, he could get in and out of the room easily. Only her dark head showed above the bedclothes. He went into the bathroom, where his pyjamas were on a hanger behind the door, warm with the rays of a wall heater, and his slippers were by the stool. This was another refinement; he would be less likely to disturb Janet if he changed here!

He was in bed within ten minutes; asleep almost at once. Snoring lightly very soon.

Professor Oliver Clayton was still under sedation but vaguely aware of light, and of being conscious. A police officer sat in a corner of his private ward; a nurse or doctor looked in at regular intervals.

Rosamund Clayton did not really sleep, but dozed; both of her daughters were with her, in a room they had shared since childhood, and each slept soundly.

Hubert Fellowes, also under sedation, was in a ward for two people in the Charing Cross Hospital, but the other bed was empty. He had undergone the same operation as Clayton, carried out by the same surgeons. He was utterly oblivious; only the oxygen tent kept him alive.

Helen, his wife, slept fitfully in a small room at her mother-in-law's apartment. Lady Fellowes, under strong advice, had taken a double-strength sleeping pill, and was fast asleep in a bigger room across the passage.

Ida Spray slept as fitfully as Helen, never for more than a few minutes at a time. In fact she did not think she really slept at all because in her waking moments she was as clear-minded as if she had been wide awake all the time. She could picture Kevin in his rage, and Oliver in his agony and now at death's door; she could 'see' the face of the policeman who had called to see her: Superintendent West, referred to in some of the newspapers as 'Handsome' West. He was certainly that! Thought of him actually made her smile. Occasionally, a vivid picture of Oliver's wife would come into her mind, too; the lovely, lovely Rosamund who must now know such anguish.

Would she ever know the whole truth?

Would the police tell her why her husband had been attacked? Simply because he had gone to the police about the blackmail?

And Kevin—under arrest!

He wasn't really, she knew; he was being questioned 'because' a radio news broadcast had said 'he might be able to help the police in their investigations'. That wasn't possible, it couldn't be possible, it *mustn't* be possible!

Only when she was thinking of Kevin and the possibility that he had been one of the two men who had attacked Oliver, did she feel real distress, and, partly because of the sleeping pills she had taken, even that was not so acute as it had been. There was at the back of her mind another realisation: she had been shocked and horrified by news of the attack on Oliver, but her real concern was not for him, only for her son. The years had brought acceptance of the situation and had strengthened affection but the love she had once felt for him had gone.

It did not realy matter whether he lived or died.

What mattered was that Kevin should not be proved guilty of attacking him.

In one of her deeper sleeping spells, the telephone bell rang. At first it startled her, and she did not know what it was but gradually the persistent ringing found its way into her consciousness. The telephone—*Kevin!* She sat up in bed and switched on the bedside light, then snatched up the telephone: who else would call her in these small hours?

She cried into the telephone: "Kevin!"

After a moment of silence, a man said: "No, I'm not Kevin, but the police have let him go."

"Oh, thank God!" she cried. "Where is he? Who is that? Where—"

"Take it easy," the caller said, with a laugh in his voice. "I'm a friend of Kevin, but he wouldn't think so if he knew I was calling you. He doesn't feel so proud of you as he did."

"Where is he?" she demanded.

"Listen to me," said the caller, "he's asleep and he's safe. He's going back to Scotland Yard to answer more questions in the morning, and it wouldn't surprise me if they keep him next time."

"Why are you telling me all this?" Ida demanded in a high-pitched voice.

"Just a friend," the man replied. "If you want to get evidence that will prove your son is innocent and save him from being sent to prison for life, you'd better get a move on."

"Where is he?" she cried.

"Meet me at the all night café at the Strand Corner House at half-past six," the man ordered. "I'll be wearing a green suit, and I've got red hair. I'll be at the counter, just inside—just come and sit next to me. I'll keep the place for you with a raincoat. Do you understand all that?"

"Yes, but—"

"Where are you to come?"

She answered breathlessly: "The Strand Corner House, at the all night café, you'll be at the counter in a green suit, and you've got red hair. But—"

The man said: "Just come. And if you want to help Kevin, don't tell a soul."

He hung up on her.

She kept the receiver to her ear and cried "Hallo, hallo!" several times but there was no response. Slowly, reluctantly, she put the receiver down. Her heart was beating wildly, and suddenly she shivered. A button at the neck of her nightdress had slipped free as she had stretched for the telephone, and the white mounds of her breasts showed: beautifully. She shivered again and clutched at the nightdress, fastened the button, and then stretched forward for a woolly wrap, which she pulled around her shoulders. Questions, most half-formed, crowded her mind. She was both frightened and hopeful; and she was wary, not knowing what was the best thing to do.

She knew she wouldn't get to sleep again. What time was it? She had pushed the bedside clock over as she had reached for the telephone, and now she straightened it and exclaimed: "Half-past five!" She scrambled out of bed, and pulled back the curtains; the first pale light of the new day was spreading over the rooftops, enough to show smoke curling from some chimneys; even to show the chimney stacks and the slate roofs.

"I haven't much time," she said feverishly.

She put on a dressing gown, made of beautifully soft Australian merino wool, a Christmas gift from a few years ago, from Oliver. She thrust her small, nicely-shaped feet into fur-lined slippers, and went to the kitchen, put on the kettle and busied herself for a few minutes in the bathroom, while it boiled. Then, warm and wide awake, she made the tea and took it back to the bedroom. She did not drive a car in London, and would have to go by bus or taxi to the Strand Corner House. Would there be any taxis about at this hour? And what time did the buses start?

Why should this 'friend' of Kevin want to meet her?

Why—why would Kevin telephone?

It was all very peculiar, and as she drank the scalding hot tea she seemed to hear the policeman's voice: "If anything is at all strange, or anything unusual happens, and if you hear from your son, let me know." God alone knew, this was strange! But Kevin had been caught, and it was too early for 'Handsome' West to be in his office. She began to dress quickly, in a smooth-textured trouser suit of bottle green; she hadn't the figure for trousers but she loved their warmth. It was nearly six

142

o'clock when she was ready to go, and she thought, almost in panic: I'll be late! Then, she thought: nothing can happen to me in a place like the Corner House. By night as well as by day there were always people there.

She went out, and into the street. It wasn't until she closed the front door that she realised that she should have called a taxi by telephone. She hurried towards Holborn, the nearest main thoroughfare, looking in all directions and down every street for a taxi.

A small private car passed her.

A motor-cycle engine roared, from a side street, so startling her that she swung round. A motor-cyclist with a crash helmet and goggles was only fifty or sixty yards behind her, roaring nearer. Quite suddenly, simply because of this, she felt an awful surge of panic and began to run.

She did not see the small car which swung out of the next side street, for she was in blind panic.

She heard the roar of the motor-cycle engine and the hum of the car, and suddenly a shout, a high-pitched whistle followed by the wail of a police siren. She stopped running, and turned. The car which had just passed her was slewed across the roadway, and the motor-cyclist, trying to mount the pavement in order to get past it, crashed on his side. Half-a-dozen white balls fell from him and rolled about the roadway into the gutter. A police car, siren wailing, was approaching from the far end of this street, while the driver of the first car jumped out and ran towards the motor-cyclist.

A tall, ungainly-looking man appeared, on foot; and as he drew up he showed her his card: he was Detective Sergeant Venables, of the Metropolitan Police. In a brisk incisive voice which few of his colleagues at the Yard ever heard, he said:

"You'll be all right now, Mrs. Spray. Please tell me exactly what happened."

She hardly came up to his shoulder, and had to bend her head back in order to see him. Before she could begin to answer and

143

before he spoke again, there was a shout from further along the road, which sounded like: "Look out!" Next moment a concrete ball hurtled from the roof of a house opposite, missed Ida Spray's head by inches, and shattered into a hundred pieces when it struck the ground.

17

More Arrests

Ida gaped upwards until a dark shadow blotted out the sight of the roof, a man on it with his arm drawn back, and the morning sky. The sergeant flung his arms around her and almost smothered her as he lifted and carried her into the doorway of a house close by. As they reached shelter another cement ball smashed against the wall just outside. Chipping flew off, into Ida's hair, over Venables's back.

Car engines snorted and men shouted, and then a man spoke from the street by their side.

"It's all clear, Sergeant. He's on the run."

The sergeant released her from his great bear hug and looked down into her eyes; there was anxiety deep in his.

"Are you all right?" he asked anxiously.

"I—I'm okay," she answered. "Were those sons of bitches trying to kill me?"

"If they weren't, the sergeant did his stuff for nothing," the other man said jocularly, and then actually backed a pace because of the expression in Venables's eyes. "Just my joke, Sarge. They were after you all right, lady."

Venables looked along the road, spotted a car with the word 'Police' on the windscreen some fifty yards away, and said: "Get that car nearer, I want to call Mr. West." The man hurried off, and Venables looked hard at the woman and went on: "Why did you come out so early?"

She explained, quite simply.

"It's a good job Mr. West told us to watch you night and day," said Venables. He did not add that it was also a good job that he, after waking early, had decided to come and see the precautions for himself; even luckier, that he had come here before he had checked the Fellowes' home.

The police car pulled up and he moved towards it. He seemed reluctant to let go of Ida Spray.

Janet West heard the telephone before Roger, who was on one side and sleeping heavily. She was tempted to let it ring, but that would serve no purpose, so she pushed back the bedclothes. Brr-brr! the bell went and Roger stirred. It was chilly. She shivered and drew a dressing gown round her shoulders as she went round the two beds and plucked up the instrument.

"This is Janet West."

"Er—ah—" a man began and she knew at once that it was Detective Sergeant Venables, to whom Roger had taken a great liking in the past few months. "I'm sorry to disturb you. I—er—and Mr. West, but—"

"Who is it?" Roger asked in a husky whisper. His eyes were wide open now and he was looking straight at her.

". . . something's happened I think he—I—"

"Venables."

"Gimme," Roger said, hoisting himself up to a sitting position. Janet handed him the telephone and watched him for a moment, then moved away, but he spoke and gripped her wrist at the same moment. "Where?" he demanded. "Where is she? . . . What? . . . Have you sent someone to the Corner House? . . . No, I wouldn't expect anyone to be there, either, but there might be . . . What's the time? . . ."

As he talked, Roger's hand slid up Janet's arm. The dressing-gown was only loose over her shoulders and she wore a short-sleeved nightdress. He was touching the warm flesh of her shoulder and she felt herself sitting down on the side of the bed;

146

relaxing. "Well, I can't get there, so you take her along and let her go in and see if this redhead in the green suit *is* waiting for her . . . Eh? All right, redheaded man . . . Will Mrs. Spray— here, let me talk to her."

He shifted his arm to Janet's waist, and brought her closer to him, although all his attention seemed to be on what he was saying.

"Hallo, Mrs. Spray, I'm sorry you had a bad fright . . . What I want you to do is to go to the Strand Corner House and do exactly what the man told you to . . . *He* may not be the one who arranged the attack on you, someone else may have overheard the conversation and it could be an invaluable help . . . You can rely absolutely on Sergeant Venables . . . Yes . . . Go ahead, Venables, but make sure nothing can happen to her or to the man, if he's there."

Roger rang off on a faint sound in Janet's ears; it sounded like: "I won't, sir." He eased himself over to one side and put his telephone arm round her, drawing her down towards him.

"Good morning, darling," he said.

"Good morning, great detective."

"Ah, there are advantages in being a Chief Superintendent," Roger said. "Occasionally you can tell someone else to get on with the job while you do what you want to do yourself."

"When, for instance?" Janet asked.

"Now, for instance," he said, and with a twist of his strong body and arms he lay by her side while she was on her back, head raised a little in the crook of his left elbow. "How long is it since I told you you were a very beautiful woman?"

She didn't answer; just smiled, showing a glint of teeth. His heart began to beat very fast, and he kissed her lightly on the lips. She was as beautiful as when they had first married. More mature but just as lovely. The suntan gave her a glow she hadn't had before they left home, while the rest and the excitement of the trip had put a glow into her eyes.

"And desirable," he said, placing his right hand on her waist.

"Darling, Richard might come in."

"You haven't known Richard to wake up before his alarm goes at seven-fifteen for weeks—months," corrected Roger hastily. "I like these shortie nighties. I can see how shapely and brown your legs are." He drew the hem an inch or two higher. "Now if my memory serves me, there remains on that body delectable of yours a narrow, a very narrow strip of the original genuine paleface skin. Well, pale skin. I think I want to find out if the tan is fading."

He kissed her again, still gently but lingeringly.

He kissed her again, less gently . . .

There was no man with red hair and a green suit in the all night café at the Corner House. Venables allowed Mrs. Spray to wait there for half-an-hour before going and joining her. She had recovered from both shock and disappointment well, and was finishing bacon and eggs and toast.

"Coffee, please," Venables ordered when a Pakistani girl came up for his order.

"You must be hungry," Ida said.

"Hm, hmm," Venables agreed.

"I was famished," Ida said. "I'd like some more toast and coffee. It wasn't until I sat down that I realized I haven't really eaten anything to say eaten since the night before last." She smiled at the girl who brought the coffee and ordered more toast, and: "Bacon and eggs for you, Sergeant?"

"Well, jolly good, thanks," Venables said. "But I mustn't be too long eating them." He signalled to a Yard man in the doorway and went on: "Anyone who wants to have breakfast now can—we'll give the red-haired man another twenty minutes."

"Right, sir!" the other said, and went and told two others who had followed him and Ida Spray here. He passed on the message, and added: "That's the same kind of thing Handsome always does—makes sure we don't kick our heels while he eats. That Sergeant Venables is going places, if you ask me."

Roger entered his office later in the morning as Venables opened the communicating door, and the outside telephone bell and the internal telephone bell rang simultaneously. Venables, filling the doorway, mouthed a name Roger understood only too well: "Coppell." The internal call was probably the Commander. He lunged forward and picked up the receiver, barking:

"West."

"Come to my office at once," Coppell said. "Drop everything else."

"Right," Roger said, and put down one receiver and picked up the other. "West."

"There's a Lady Fellowes on the line, sir."

"Hold her on one moment," Roger said, and swung to Venables. "Any news of Hubert Fellowes?"

"Still hanging on."

"Professor Clayton?"

"Much improved."

"Any word from Mrs. Spooner—of Gooden's?"

"No, sir."

"Call her home number and ask her if she has her report ready," Roger ordered.

"Sir, the Commander—"

"*Hurry!* Put Lady Fellowes through now, please." Roger watched Venables dodge back to his own room; the door slammed as a woman spoke. "Good morning, Lady Fellowes." Roger put as much warmth into his voice as he could. "I'm glad that your son had a reasonable night."

"Mr. West, I want to talk to you, urgently." She sounded almost breathless.

"Of course. Can you come here to the Yard?"

"No. I would like to meet you somewhere privately."

"Where do you suggest?" Roger asked. He heard Venables talking in the next room, he was thinking as hard as he could, he was anxious not to upset Coppell but the job was more important.

"I—I really don't know. Unless—"

"Yes?"

"My club, or—perhaps the Savoy, or—"

"Much too public," Roger said, "but I would *very* much like to see you. Do you know Hampstead well?"

"Very well."

"I have to be there about eleven o'clock. Can you be at the White Stone Pond by Jack Straw's Castle?"

"Oh, yes," Lady Fellowes answered. "Yes!" She sounded breathless with gratitude. "Eleven o'clock at White Stone Pond at Hampstead Heath, then!"

"Thank you," Roger said. "Forgive me now, but I'm in a wild hurry." He rang off and looked up as Venables came in. "Has Mrs. Spooner—"

"She said she stayed up half the night finishing her report," Venables replied, "and I suggested that she should bring it straight here, to you."

"When?"

"She expects to arrive about ten o'clock."

"Do fine," Roger said, and the inter-office telephone began to ring again. "Come on," he urged, "let it ring. You come and tell me all about Ida Spray and anything else on the way to the Commander's office."

"He's been after you since eight o'clock," Venables said, breathlessly.

"And it's now eight-thirty, so I haven't been snuggling abed," Roger said as they swung into the passage. "Have any of the Hokki Braves talked?"

"No, sir."

"Where's Kevin Spray?"

"We lost him, sir."

"He'd better turn up at ten o'clock or somebody's head will roll," Roger growled. "When?"

"Last night."

"Did he give our chaps the slip?"

"Yes, sir. Someone came after him with a motor-cycle, must have been watching, and he went off on the pillion."

"Right." They were halfway to Coppell's office, taking long strides. "Were all the men who attacked Mrs. Spray Hokki Braves?"

"They all had membership cards, sir."

"Cards?"

"A piece of raw-hide leather, sir, with the letters H.B. burned on it in Japanese characteristics."

"Branded," Roger said. "How many Hokki camps are there in the country?"

"The latest total known according to Hokki distributors is four hundred and seventy-one, sir."

"And how many at the universities?"

"All except Cambridge and one or two red-bricks—forty-one."

"Any more drugs found?"

"No, sir, but there's one good thing. We've found where those cement balls are made."

"Thank God for that!" exclaimed Roger. "Where?"

"In an old builder's yard in Kennington," Venables answered. "There's an old mould there from a small cement factory that was dismantled and demolished a few months ago. The moulds were made for cement wall decoration. And there are some motor-cycle tracks in the yard."

"Have it watched," urged Roger, and gripped Venables's arm. "Get back to the office and be at the end of a telephone. Better have someone else in there with you, in case you need a messenger."

"I will, sir!"

They were within a few feet of Coppell's door when it opened and Coppell strode out, glowering, and saying over his shoulder:

"I'll get him here if I have to drag him by the scruff of the neck!" Then he missed a step as Roger froze to attention; they came within inches of colliding. Venables turned, and fled. Roger put on his most formal smile, and said:

"Good morning, sir."

"About time," Coppell growled. He pushed the door back into his office and over his shoulder Roger could see the Assistant Commissioner, Colonel Frobisher, who had a settled-in look; what had brought both Frobisher and the Commander in so early? And what had put Coppell in such a mood?

"Good morning, Superintendent," the Assistant Commissioner said. He looked very tired; lean and fit but with red-rimmed eyes which had dark shadows under them.

"Good morning, sir."

Coppell closed the door, and it slammed; it had never before occurred to Roger that there was anything in common between the Commander and Venables, but he had a sudden thought: that much of Coppell's attitude might be due to a basic insecurity; that was certainly Venables's main problem.

What the blazes was he thinking about 'insecurity' for?

"Handsome," Coppell growled, "we've been taken for a ride. We've been led by the nose to those Hokki Braves, or whatever they call themselves, so that we wouldn't see what was really going on. Did you realise that?"

"No," Roger said, "but I've considered the possibility, sir. I'd got as far as being sure these motor-cyclists were being used to make us concentrate on the wrong lead, though. There are nearly five hundred clubs in the country, with an average membership of fifty, say twenty-five thousand riders. It wouldn't make sense that we had twenty-five thousand incipient or active criminals in the organisation for direct blackmailing unless it were on a stupendous scale. So, I've wondered what alternative there could be: possibly that they are being used to keep us busy and away from the main causes of the crimes."

"D'you know what for?" growled Coppell.

152

"No," answered Roger. "I only know that Fellowes, Gooden and Aker were driven to suicide, but the more I hear the more I doubt whether one of them would have killed himself rather than tell his wife. This is hindsight, sir—after getting to know Lady Fellowes and studying reports about the attitudes of the other men's wives. The motivation seemed convincing at first sight but less so now. But there could still be a common factor and we have a visit to Australia as a possibility. I'm now assuming that Professor Clayton and Hubert Fellowes were attacked for the same reason as the others committed suicide, and that an early morning attempt today on the life of Mrs. Spray, Clayton's mistress, as well as the attacks on me are all for the same reason, too."

"What reason?" roared Coppell.

"I don't like guessing but it could be to prevent us from talking about what we know or suspect," answered Roger.

"Ah," intervened Frobisher, speaking for the first time, "what is it that you know in common with these people, Superintendent?" He held up a long, thin hand to stop Coppell from interrupting, as he went on: "The Home Secretary, in common with other members of the Cabinet, is gravely concerned. I have spent most of the night in conferences and discussions. We have received anonymous information which is most disturbing. These reports imply that there will be a widespread series of raids on banks and post offices today—*today*," he repeated with almost sinister emphasis. "The information further implies that you have wrongly led us to believe that these Hokki Braves should be given priority, and that the police forces throughout the country will be distracted by the motor-cyclists while other men, not remotely concerned with the motor-cyclists, will carry out the other raids.

"Further, Chief Superintendent, our information is that you have reason to suspect this. If you have, why haven't you informed the Commander?"

The Assistant Commissioner's voice was as sharp and cold as

153

the cutting edge of a carving knife, but Coppell was staring at Roger with a strange and completely unfamiliar expression in his eyes. It was as if he were pleading with Roger not only to deny the accusation but to justify his denial.

18

Accusation

The Assistant Commissioner's face seemed to grow longer; his jaw more lantern; the mouth smaller; the eyes, accusing. And for a few moments he was all Roger could see; he was oblivious of Coppell and of the room; the bright blue sky and the reflection from something bright, outside. He felt quite sure that the man took this seriously; was already more than half-convinced that the reports were right; that he, Chief Detective Superintendent Roger West, was betraying the trust he had earned over the years.

At first, he felt anger, even fury, welling up inside him. That did not last long, for the absurdity of the charge—and in effect it was a charge—began to strike home. It was absurd both against the background of this particular case and against his record at the Yard.

He began to smile.

Anger reflected in the Assistant Commissioner's eyes, but the harder he considered the situation the funnier it seemed and the smile grew almost into a grin. He considered what to say, knowing only that he must get his word in first; and as the other's lips began to move, as if he were going to speak again, he said in a casual voice which had a hint of laughter in it:

"So that's what they've been up to!"

"Explain yourself," demanded the Assistant Commissioner, coldly.

"Well, sir, I don't know of a single thing that has made me dangerous to anybody, but the obvious reason for these people to try to kill me was to silence me. I couldn't think why, but there had to be a reason, and that bothered me badly. Now, I think I can see what they've been up to. They've made a good job of making it appear that I do know something, or you wouldn't be so disturbed, sir. Where did the information come from?"

"Most reliable sources," the Assistant Commissioner replied sharply.

"But who, sir?"

"I don't propose to vouchsafe—" began Frobisher.

"Bloody unfair," growled Coppell, not glaring but looking nervous. "Accuse a man of West's calibre and then refuse to say who's been framing—accusing him." He averted his gaze and muttered again under his breath: "That's bloody unfair in my book."

It was not the first time that Coppell, who was such a difficult man to deal with, was often a bully, utterly unreasonable, far too demanding, had taken Roger's side in a conflict with the V.I.Ps. Roger warmed to him; but the frosty expression in the Assistant Commissioner's eyes did nothing to suggest that he had even begun to thaw.

"This information was confidential."

"Fascinating," interrupted Roger. "Almost the first word I heard in this case was 'confidential'. It doesn't really matter whether you name your informant, sir—no case could possibly be proved against me. The charge is utterly false. But there is a lot of evidence that the criminals involved are working against time. If they could kill, or even get me removed from the case for a few days, apparently, it would help them." He pushed back his chair and banged a clenched fist into the palm of his other hand. "But *how?* And *why?*"

"I do not find this very convincing," the Assistant Commissioner declared. "A display of histrionics is hardly an answer to the suggestion implied in my information."

Roger looked at him and said: "No, I suppose not, sir. I would like to ask whether you have any evidence to support your charges?"

"No charge has been made," Frobisher retorted. "But in view of the information lodged with me I do not think it advisable that you should continue in your investigations until I am fully satisfied that the information is false. I wish you to hand the assignment over to another officer, Chief Superintendent. Commander, will you make the necessary arrangements?"

To Roger, it was like a blow in the face and a kick in the stomach at the same time: he felt sick. Until that moment he had thought Frobisher was deliberately pushing to make him talk if in fact he was keeping information, but there was now no doubt at all: Frobisher wanted him off the case. He watched the new Assistant Commissioner with great intentness, while Coppell breathed very heavily, as if he could find no words to combat this.

"At once," Frobisher ordered.

Coppell drew in a great heaving breath, stood up from his chair, and said hoarsely: "No, I won't."

"What?"

"I won't take West off this case unless you can give me some evidence that he's unlawfully involved," Coppell declared stubbornly. "I don't think it's right and I don't think it will get results. Handsome—" He drew in another deep breath, but seemed to be less worried by the stand he was taking. "Are you sure you don't know why they want you off the case so urgently?"

"No," Roger said. "I'm not sure—but I'm not absolutely sure of anything. I want to talk to—"

"Commander," interrupted the Assistant Commissioner, "I do not wish to use my authority to suspend you as well—"

157

"You haven't got any such authority," Coppell interrupted. "There's only one man who has, and that's the Commissioner."

"He is out of town. His authority is vested in me, and—"

Coppell said, heavily: "Colonel Frobisher, you're new to the Yard and you don't know how we work. I believe in West, and if West is taken off the case over my head, my resignation goes with it, whether the Commissioner gives the order or you go to the Home Secretary because the Commissioner's away. Is that what you want?" He glowered, at least as authoritative with Frobisher as with any man under him. "If you want us both out on our necks, I would need a Home Office order signed by the Home Secretary himself."

"Then that is exactly what I shall get." Frobisher pulled his chair back. "You will be ill-advised to take any action until I return." He turned towards the door, and opened it.

Coppell watched him go, and then wiped the back of his thick, red neck.

"I don't know where the hell this is going to end," he growled. "I hope to God you know what you're doing. If you don't he'll probably have both our heads. *Do* you know?"

"I know what I want to do," Roger said.

"What's that?"

"Have every owner of a Hokki motor-cycle who is also a member of the Hokki Braves questioned by their local police," Roger said. "I don't know what is being planned but we can't rule out the possibility that the members of this club are in it as deep as they can go. And we can't rule out the possibility that approaching the suicides as if they had the same motivation is causing the trouble."

"But—" began Coppell.

"Commander," Roger said. "Kevin Spray is supposed to come and see me again at ten o'clock. Lady Fellowes has asked me to meet her at eleven o'clock. Mrs. Spooner, Sir Jeremy Gooden's secretary, is also due to come and see me in the next hour. I've hardly time to breathe."

158

Coppell stood massive and menacing behind his desk.

"If it weren't for me you wouldn't be able to do a damned thing," he said.

"And if the A.C. gets that authority to override you, sir, neither of us will." Roger threw up his hands. "I simply haven't time to tell you how grateful I am, how—"

"Get to hell out of here," rasped Coppell. "And don't come and see me again until you know what it's all about. I'll see to those Hokki owners."

What I need, thought Roger, is time; and time is the one thing I haven't got.

He walked back to his office, slowly for him; it was a little after nine, and almost incredible that so much could have happened in half-an-hour. He could just hear Venables, who was presumably on the telephone. He went to his window and looked out, disappointed by grey roofs, by the fact that he didn't get a glimpse of the Thames and Westminster Bridge. What an odd thing the mind was; it was three years since they had left the old building and he had momentarily forgotten that: the crisis had jolted him so badly.

He stood absolutely still, willing his mind to work.

There must be a key to this; there was always a key; once he had it he would be able to open the door and see everything beyond. Was the key really in his hand? Or had he come into the affair too late? At times he thought he had sparked off the action but—had he? It had started with Aker, and he hadn't even got round to seeing the aeronautical engineer's wife yet. Gooden had killed himself two weeks ago, but Fellowes only two days ago. So he himself hadn't begun a thing. It was conceivable that when he had talked to Professor Clayton he had started the wheels humming, but Clayton had come to him, he hadn't gone to Clayton. The first person he had gone to see was Ida Spray.

Odd name: Spray. Was it her real name?

What common factor could there be? Apart from the infidelity, which was hardly a rarity among men. Look for the common factors. One: three men had committed suicide. But only three—Clayton hadn't, nor had young Fellowes; so the suicides were not common factors in all cases. Look again. What did the three men who had died by their own hand have in common with those who had been attacked? List them: Sir Douglas Fellowes, Sir Jeremy Gooden, Norman Aker, Professor Clayton, Hubert Fellowes and he, Roger West. Should one count threats? If so, then young and pretty Helen Fellowes must be added to the list.

He, Roger, had absolutely *nothing* in common with the others, so could he forget this general approach?

Or *did* he in fact share some knowledge, without realising it? Was shared knowledge which someone wanted to keep secret the common factor? If so, what did he know that the others could have known?

Silly question! How could he possibly tell?

Remember, it might be staring me in the face, he thought. And don't forget that a very strong attempt has been made to discredit me. They, whoever they are, could not kill or put me out of action, so they tried to discredit me. They did a damned good job, too. Frobisher doesn't trust me as far as he can see me, only Coppell gave me breathing space. Whoever thought the day would come again when I would bless the name of Coppell.

Aloud, he gasped: "My God!"

A simple truth which he had missed, or the significance of which had not dawned on him, now came with thumping force. For the information which had so affected Frobisher must have come from somewhere very high up in the Government or Civil Service. Frobisher was utterly convinced. He was getting most of his briefs from the Home Office, the Ministry which controlled all Home Affairs. Was there someone highly placed in the Home Office who wanted to discredit him, Roger?

They couldn't hope to discredit him for long, so they must have a short term purpose in mind. Something *was* going to happen quickly, and possibly today. He moved for the first time

160

since taking up his stance by the window, went to the inter-office telephone and called *Information*.

"Is there a general call out for Hokki owners?" he demanded.

"Nationwide," the Inspector-in-charge answered. "It came from the Commander himself, and all regional and provincial forces are co-operating."

"Thanks," Roger said, and rang off. Thank God for Coppell! What did all the people involved have in common—what did Ida Spray know, for instance, which had made the other side want her dead? Lord, he hadn't seen her yet and she had been down in a waiting-room for ages. He went to the communicating door and found Venables in his shirt sleeves, looking sweaty hot as he banged a typewriter with astounding speed. He jumped at the sound of Roger's voice.

"Sir."

"Is Mrs. Spooner here yet?"

"In Waiting Room 3, sir. Mrs. Spray's next door."

"I'm going down straight away. If I'm not back when Kevin Spray arrives, let me know he's here and keep him in your office."

"Very good, sir."

"Has any of the prisoners talked?"

"Not a solitary word," Venables answered. "They're being pulled into police stations all over the country. You knew that, didn't you?"

"Yes." How he knew it!

"Won't be room to hold them all. There's over a hundred from London University alone."

"There'll be room," Roger said. "What are you hammering away at?"

"My report on what happened this morning at the Corner House, sir—I never like to get behind if I can help it."

"You don't have to tell me, David." It was seldom that he used the other's Christian name. "What do I know that I don't realise?"

"About this case, sir?"

"Yes."

"Something in your subconscious I daresay, sir. I—ah—I—er —I *have* been wondering what all the victims might have in common," went on Venables, gathering both speed and courage when Roger waited for him to continue. "I did come across one thing but I expect you've thought about it."

"I haven't turned up a thing," Roger said. "Let's have it."

"*Really*, sir?"

"And don't stand there thinking how clever you are!"

"No, sir! Well, sir. It—well, it *couldn't* have anything to do with the case, sir, could it, but—well—" *For the love of Mike let it come*, Roger almost pleaded. "Well, you have all travelled, sir."

"What?"

"Travelled. Gone places—especially in the Far East and the Antipodes, come to think of it. Sir Douglas Fellowes was in New Zealand and Australia, Sir Jeremy Gooden in Tokyo which isn't far from Australia, Mr. Akers is always flying all over the world, and he did some test flying for a new Australian aircraft only ten days ago, Mrs. Spray's been to Australia, hasn't she, and so has Professor Clayton, and—er—ah—well, sir, you and Mrs. West had a trip to Africa, and you did have some long side trips." Venables gulped, and then made himself go on: "I expect it's sheer coincidence, but someone might think you were following in their footsteps, so to speak, mightn't they?"

"David," Roger said, huskily, "check everything you know about all the victims. Where they've been, when, and for what ostensible reason, in the past six months."

"Oh, I've got that done, sir," said Venables, "but—hang it, I threw the notes in the wastepaper-basket! I hope to heaven—" He stooped down, missed the edge of his desk by a fraction, and then cried out in triumph: "It hasn't been emptied, it's here somewhere! I'll have it typed out again by the time you get back. But one thing's certain—*all* the others have been to Australia within the past year."

162

19

The Three Women

Roger said to Venables: "I may call in for it. And get some copies done—up to a dozen." He turned back to his own office, his heart beating like a trip hammer, and with a twist of nausea in his stomach. He pulled the internal telephone towards him and dialled a number opposite the entry: *Commander, Uniform.* A woman answered on the instant.

"Commander McReady's office."

"If the Commander is there I would like a word with him," Roger said. "This is Chief Superintendent West, C.I.D."

"One moment, Mr. West." Her voice faded but did not die until a man's, with a faint Scottish burr, replaced it.

McReady, of *Uniform,* was known as one of the most efficient men at the Yard, one who had every job at his fingertips; and his job was to have men available to help with crowd control, traffic, a great variety of things which were only indirectly the concern of the C.I.D.

"You've given us quite a job this morning," he said. "How many of these Hokki Braves do you think we'll pick up?"

"About a hundred in the university area, sir," Roger answered. "But with luck we won't have to hold many for long. Can you give me some information about the Annual Conference of the Anthropologists or whatever they're called, at the British Museum?"

"Not strictly speaking at the Museum Halls," replied

McReady, going on with a laugh in his voice: "The Old Fossils meet in the Halls, close by the museum. In fact there's an entrance from the main museum building to the Halls themselves. Why?"

"What time do their sessions begin?"

"Ten o'clock, and they are prompt. There are usually a number of committee meetings which will be starting about now. They—" McReady caught his breath and stopped, while Roger thought: 'Old Fossils.' "Chief Superintendent," McReady went on in a much less relaxed voice. "Professor Clayton was to have attended the conference. Have you any reason to believe the attack on him was concerned with that?"

"I've the beginning of an idea that it might have been," Roger said. "He was to have delivered an important paper."

"It's still on the agenda," said McReady.

"They can't hope that he'll be well enough to read it!" Roger gasped.

"According to the word I had with the museum security chaps last night, they think someone will read it for him," McReady said. "Mrs. Clayton apparently knows where it is. They're very punctilious, and run their meetings better than most. West—"

"He could have been attacked to prevent him from reading the paper," Roger said. "How many men will you have there, sir?"

"One inside, part of the time. Two outside, when the sessions begin and end. Many of the delegates stay in Bloomsbury hotels, and walk; it isn't exactly a major problem. But there's a lot of traffic about the university about the same time."

"I want to send several men along to mix with the crowd going in, and to slip one or two into the meeting hall. I'll be most grateful for your help."

"No need to be. I'll see that my chaps are alerted to expect yours."

"Thank you very much, sir."

"But West, do you seriously expect trouble?"

"I think there's enough to warrant us being extremely careful. Have you any idea who they think will read the paper?"

"They don't appear to have named anyone."

"Who would be likely to know?"

"The Chairman and the Secretary of the Conference," McReady said. "Give me a moment and I'll let you have the telephone number at the Halls." There was a murmur of voices before he came back: "Bloomsbury 81751."

"Thanks," Roger said, and then with even greater warmth: "Very many thanks indeed, sir!" He rang off on McReady's: "I hope you've got something," and almost immediately put in a call through the operator to the Halls. He waited for the call to come through, looking at the electric clock on the wall. It was twenty-past nine. How long was he going to have to wait? Should he go to the waiting-rooms, and take it there? He was half-out of his seat when the telephone bell rang and a man with a deep, gruff voice announced:

"This is Professor Considine, of the Anthropological Society Conference."

"Good morning, Professor," Roger said. "This is Chief Super-intendent West of Scotland Yard."

"Indeed," said Considine, as if he doubted it.

"I've been told you may have Professor Clayton's paper read this morning," Roger said. "Can you confirm that, and tell me who is to read it, please?"

There was a long and unexpected silence, until the other man replied: "Most certainly not. How do *I* know you are a police officer? This is a confidential matter and I shall certainly give no information over the telephone."

Roger had time to collect himself as the man was talking, and in his most matter-of-fact voice, he suggested:

"Will you call New Scotland Yard, sir—you'll find the number listed—and ask for Chief Superintendent West? That way you can be quite sure you are talking to a police officer."

"I have no desire to impart this information to the police,

from whom it would almost certainly leak to the newspapers. Professor Clayton had a report of the greatest significance to make, in *confidence*."

"Professor Considine," protested Roger, "this could be a matter of great urgency."

The Professor hung up on him.

Roger put his own receiver back, almost unbelievingly. It was now half-past nine, there was so little time. He could ring McReady again, or—

The communicating door opened, and Venables appeared; not a triumphant Venables with the list in his hands but a troubled Venables who had something to say which he knew Roger would not like. He held onto the door jamb, as if for support.

"Well?" Roger demanded.

"Kevin Spray won't be here at ten o'clock," Venables announced.

"Why? Has anything happened—"

"He's not hurt, sir—he's been picked up in Paris. He slipped our men in London and crossed the Channel wearing a false beard and moustache last night, and was picked up at the Gare du Nord when he thought he was safe and had discarded the disguise. By a bit of luck one of our chaps was on the train, he'd gone over to see the Sûreté Nationale about that big art theft from Chelsea, and recognised him. He just telephoned, sir."

"Ask the Paris police to hold him. We'll send for him this morning."

"I've already—yes, sir."

"Have you heard from the men watching Professor Clayton's house?" asked Roger.

"Not this morning, sir."

"Check at once. Tell them I want to know if Mrs. Clayton leaves, and I want her followed if she does. Then telephone the Chief of Security at the British Museum and find out if he can tell us when and by whom Professor Clayton's paper is going to be read. Let me know at once whatever the answer. I'm going down to see Mrs. Spooner and Mrs. Spray, then going to Hampstead where I want to talk to Mrs. Clayton, and I've an eleven o'clock rendezvous with Lady Fellowes at the White Stone Pond, Hampstead."

"You'll never do it all, sir!"

"And find out how Kevin Spray got across the Channel."

"We know he picked up the train from Dunquerque, the overnight ferry train—"

"And we know he didn't have time to catch the train from Victoria," Roger said. He was already at the door. "One other thing: if the Commander or the Assistant Commissioner wants me you don't know where I am. You know who I'm going to see, but haven't any idea of my itinerary. All understood?"

"Yes, sir," Venables said, meekly.

Roger went out like the wind. Everything went right for a few moments; a lift was at his landing, open and empty; it took him to the second floor, where an elderly uniformed officer was waiting.

"Which room is Mrs. Spooner in?" Roger asked.

"Room One, sir."

"Thanks. Alone?"

"Oh yes, sir."

Roger had a glimpse of the 'battleaxe' through the one way window. She was spilling over on either side of an armchair, and her mouth drooped open; she appeared to be sleeping the sleep of exhaustion; and of the righteous. She didn't stir as Roger went in, saying to the orderly: "Tell Mrs. Spray I'll be with her in a few minutes, will you?"

"Yes, sir."

On a table by the side of the chair was a large envelope, open; and on it were two words: Superintendent West. He opened it, and began to read the report. Sir Jeremy Gooden's *affaire* was of long standing; this report gave the dates, the name of the woman concerned, whose name was Cassidy; Jane Cassidy; where she lived, how often Gooden had visited her. Never had there been a more confidential secretary than Elizabeth Spooner, who stirred, and began to snore gently.

"Mrs. Spooner!" Roger raised his voice but went on reading. Three months ago Gooden had gone to Tokyo, Australia and New Zealand to visit associated banks. *J.C. flew to Sydney, N.S.W., two days after J.G. left Heath Row.* So, Gooden had taken his lady love on a business trip, just as Clayton had. He called again: "Mrs. Spooner!" The snoring stopped, and he knew she was awake but ignored that for a few moments. Jane Cassidy had come home two days ahead of Gooden, they had been very careful. He had been away in all for five weeks, until seven weeks ago; early in March.

A paragraph, underlined, seemed to jump out at Roger. It read:

The first threat, the first blackmail, was on March 17th, a telephone call to the office. I listened in on the extension, as always unless specifically instructed not to. A man with a young-sounding, rather anxious voice demanded ten thousand pounds, and threatened, if he didn't get it, to send his wife a list of the hotels and motels where Gooden had stayed with his mistress during his trip.

Roger looked up, to find the deepset eyes studying him.

"And Sir Jeremy paid up," he remarked. "To the first threat, I mean."

"He was too busy and too involved to do anything else," she answered.

"And there were—" he counted swiftly. "Seven blackmail demands in all?"

"Yes."

"He paid each time—a total of forty thousand pounds."

"Yes."

"*Why*, Mrs. Spooner?"

"You know why," she replied, sharply. "He was afraid that a domestic scandal would force an investigation into his business affairs, and he had borrowed substantially from the bank, without authorisation from his fellow directors."

"Do you know why?"

"He invested the money and was confident there would be a substantial return, but he did not think his co-directors would approve of the investment—there was some degree of risk. He was always more ready to take risks than were any of the others."

"Finally, there was a demand for another ten thousand pounds. He couldn't find more money, you say."

"No," Elizabeth Spooner answered. "He simply couldn't go on. His private resources were exhausted."

"So you say in this quite remarkable report," returned Roger, but there was a dry note in his voice. "Rather than have the whole story come out, he killed himself."

"Yes. I have made that very clear."

"Was there any other reason?" asked Roger. "Had he reason to believe that the risk he had taken was too great, and he could never repay his unlawful borrowing?"

"All I know is that he said he couldn't go on," she replied. "I have told you *everything* I know." There was defiance in her eyes, and Roger thought: 'Yes, you've told me all you know but not all you guess and suspect.' There was no time to force that issue with her, and he stood up briskly. "You've been very good and I'm sorry I kept you waiting. Would you like a car to take you home?"

"No, thank you," she said. "I will walk until I get a taxi."

The last person in this room who had refused a police car lift from Roger had been Kevin Spray. He did not force this point, either, but as he moved to open the door, he asked:

"Did Sir Jeremy see Professor Clayton or Sir Douglas Fellowes in Australia?"

She stood absolutely still, and her cheeks turned crimson, for a moment her breathing became swift and shallow. Then, she retorted in a weak voice:

"I was not there, so how could I know?"

"Perhaps you would know whether he met Norman Aker?" Roger asked in his mildest voice. "And you can confirm my belief that there was no other woman in Sir Jeremy's life, that he committed suicide for some quite different reason, knowing you would lie for him when he was dead as you so often did when he was alive." This time the colour faded from her cheeks and for a moment he thought she was going to fall. But he did not want that kind of crisis, so he went on gently: "Mrs. Spooner, I strongly advise you to add the answers to those questions and other information to your report. Would you prefer to do that here, or at home?"

She stood, unsteady and uncertain. He needed more time but there wasn't more, so he went out ahead of her, and as the elderly sergeant came up, he said: "If Mrs. Spooner leaves, I want her followed. If she stays, don't disturb her." He strode along to the next doorway and opened it so suddenly that he startled Ida Spray, who was looking through a magazine. She also looked tired, but compared with the massive Mrs. Spooner, she was petite and most attractive.

"Sorry I kept you," Roger said, "and forgive me if I don't stay too long. I want—"

"Is there any news of Kevin?" she demanded.

"He left the country again last night," Roger answered, brusquely.

"*Kevin* did!" She looked as if she could not believe it; and was appalled.

"I'm afraid so," said Roger; it would do no good to be too impatient, so he made himself speak slowly. "When in Australia last year, did you and Professor Clayton meet Sir Douglas Fellowes, or Sir Jeremy Gooden, or Norman Aker, the test pilot and aeronautical engineer?"

She was as dumbfounded as Elizabeth Spooner; he had no doubt at all that Clayton had met the others, for she stood with her mouth drooping open and her hands raised in front of her bosom. Roger pushed his fingers through his hair, gave her a few moments to recover her poise, and then asked:

"Do you know why they met? What they discussed? It could be of vital importance, Mrs. Spray."

She gulped, hesitated, closed her eyes, and then suddenly opened them again and spoke with unexpected vigour. She gave the impression of being a woman of great courage and will-power.

"As they were in Australia he arranged to see them," she cried. "He had discovered some of the most astounding fossils and bones of early man, he had reason to believe he might have found the missing link. And—and they were in caves where those *heathens* were working for diamonds and gold. They wanted to blast the caves open, and that would have destroyed everything he was doing, would have destroyed vital clues to the origins of the human race. So he went to see them and told them he would tell the world if they did use dynamite in the caves. They were working secretly, you see, they didn't want any competitors to know, so—so they promised to use pick and shovel. He met them all right—he routed them!" There was the light of battle and the glow of triumph in her eyes.

"Mrs. Spray," Roger asked gently, "did he tell anyone other than you about this?"

"No! He wouldn't; he'd given his word."

"Did you tell anyone?"

She flushed to the roots of her hair, and it was a noticeable time before she shook her head and uttered her denials. But he did not believe her, and she knew it; and when she left, she was very frightened.

She accepted the offer of a police car to take her home.

By then it was ten minutes past ten. Roger called Venables, to check whether Mrs. Clayton had made any movement from her house; she had not, none of the watching policemen had seen her leave. And there was no message from the Commander. Roger went down one flight of stairs, found his own car just outside,

171

and drove off. The quickest way to Hampstead was by side streets to Hyde Park and then Regents Park: it could be one of the longest and most exasperating drives in London. This morning the fates were with him, and he pulled up outside the Clayton house in Beacon Road, Hampstead Heath, in half an hour.

Three minutes later, he was admitted to Professor Clayton's study, by Mrs. Clayton, who was dressed in dark grey, whose lovely face was pale, but who spoke with great self-confidence. The study was a bower of daffodils and jonquils; beautiful.

"I shall be glad to give you all the help I can this afternoon, Superintendent, but I can spare you only a few minutes this morning. It is ten to eleven and at eleven I must leave for a most important appointment."

"At the Museum Conference Halls?" asked Roger, quietly.

She looked startled. "Yes, but I had no idea that anyone but the Chairman of the Conference and one or two members of the committee knew that. I am going to read a paper which my husband prepared before he was attacked. It was in the safe. It has not yet been opened by anyone but my husband, and I shall have no chance to study it before reading it to the delegates. So I am sure you will understand that I am very nervous. Please do forgive me this afternoon."

20

The Old Fossils

The one thing above all that Roger needed was to find out the contents of the paper which Clayton had prepared, which she was to present to the Conference. It might be little more than Ida had already told him, and it might be of vital significance, but could it make much difference whether he saw the document before she read the whole lecture, or even whether he was present during the reading? There was no way of being sure but it seemed unbelievable that an hour could make a vital difference.

So he smiled, easily, and said: "Of course, Mrs. Clayton."

"Thank you."

"I want to ask you if you can help the inquiry by telling me of your husband's movements while in the Far East and Australia earlier in the year."

"I will do all I can," she promised.

"Thank you," he said in turn. "May I give you a lift to the Conference Halls?"

"No, thank you. My daughters are taking me," she answered, and almost on the instant a tall young woman appeared in the doorway. "Bertha, dear, see Mr. West to the door for me, will you?"

The young woman led him past the window where the sun shone vividly on the grass and the herbaceous border. At the door, which was on one side, he paused long enough to look into her young face and clear grey eyes; worried eyes.

"Will you be driving?" he asked.

"Yes."

"We don't expect any trouble, but we shall have you followed, to make sure," he told her. "Don't be surprised if you are followed very closely."

There was no doubt of the relief in her eyes.

"I won't," she promised. "It's a great help."

It was then two minutes to eleven, and Roger hurried to his car, where a detective officer stood by for instructions.

"Watch them closely," Roger ordered. "Follow close on their heels."

"We've two cars, sir, and every officer *en route* has been alerted."

"Have the grounds and approaches been searched?"

"Yes, sir."

"Good." Roger climbed into his car and started the engine. There was no message from the Yard, or he would have heard from the detective officer. He saw the two police cars and several detectives as he drove away. It was a five minutes drive to the Pond, which meant he would be five minutes late for Lady Fellowes. Almost for the first time, he allowed himself to think about her and to wonder what she wanted. He saw uniformed policemen along this road, the one which Mrs. Clayton would take; if the precautions were wasted, at least he would have nothing with which to blame himself.

He reached the Pond and saw Lady Fellowes, standing and watching a small boy pushing a tiny sailing yacht with a stick. A few cars were parked, a few people were about; he recognised two detective officers from the Yard, and a woman detective-sergeant. He pulled up as close to Lady Fellowes as he could, and as if she sensed his arrival, she turned round.

Of all the women involved in this case, she was by far the most striking; the most unusual. In conventional terms Rosamund Clayton was more beautiful, but this woman had some kind of magnetic attraction; Roger had felt it when he had first seen her and was keenly aware of it now.

"Good morning," he said.

She smiled, very faintly.

"Thank you for coming, I simply had to see you where we couldn't be overheard and without Helen knowing." They fell into step and began to walk on the grass near the Pond; none of the detectives present showed the slightest interest; they were doing a first-class job. "I was really in a dreadful quandary of divided loyalty," Lady Fellowes went on. "Between my family and—will it sound terribly smug if I say 'society'?"

"It will tell me exactly what you mean," Roger assured her.

"I hoped it would. Mr. West, we both know why my husband is supposed to have committed suicide. To me, the thought that he would rather die than tell me that he shared part of his life with another woman was ludicrous; his death was tragic and a cause of deep grief, but the reason—I simply did not believe it."

"Do you know what the real reason is?" asked Roger.

"Do *you* know there is an alternative?"

"Yes. In this day and age a man of your husband's maturity and experience would be most unlikely to take such extreme action," Roger replied. "Lady Fellowes, I've very little time."

"I will come straight to the heart of the matter," she said, quietly. "My daughter-in-law tells me that both my husband and my son were involved in some major—Helen used the word mammoth—plan which had to do with my husband's visit to Australia earlier this year. Hubert, apparently, was going to tell you about it, and Helen believes that once the police were involved he was attacked to make sure he could tell no one. It had to do with some discovery of minerals in Australia. Helen is afraid that if she or I were to tell you then Hubert might become involved in some scandal and—she is deeply in love with him, but has just been through a period of great strain." She was pleading with him not to blame Helen too much. "I have written this down for you in case—in case anything should happen to me and prevent me from testifying whenever necessary."

He stopped walking, took a sealed envelope, and stood face to face with her for a few moments; and then he said, to ease her sense of guilt: "I am sure we would have discovered this by our own efforts. It doesn't lessen my gratitude."

"You're very kind," she said.

"You are very—" he began, and checked himself; hesitated; and then left the sentence in mid-air. "I must go," he said. "You will be followed home by Yard men and carefully watched and looked after until this affair is over. It shouldn't be long."

When he drove off, she was standing and watching the small boy again.

He was only just on the move, and had not yet started down the hill to Swiss Cottage, when his radio-telephone crackled, and *Information* came on the air.

"This is Scotland Yard calling Superintendent West with an urgent message . . . This is Scotland Yard calling Superintendent West with an urgent message . . . Will Superintendent West please return as quickly as possible to his office for discussions with Commander Coppell . . . Will Superintendent West . . ."

Roger stretched out his left arm and switched the radio off.

Fifteen minutes later, envelope unopened, he pulled up close to the Conference Halls, in Euston Street; there was no room at all to park so he called a uniformed constable over, gave him an ignition key and said: "Move this if you have to." The constable took the key, uncomprehendingly. His astonished: "Superintendent West!" followed Roger down the street.

It was twenty minutes to twelve.

Security officers and police were in the entrance and in the passages leading to the main conference rooms. As he turned a corner, Roger heard Rosamund Clayton's voice quite clearly.

176

Across a wide passage were several swing doors, one of them open, with a security man and a uniformed policeman standing just inside.

They waved him through.

The doors were on the side, so newcomers could not easily distract speakers on the rostrum, yet Roger could get a good view, sideways on. Only two people were on the rostrum—an elderly, grey-bearded man, and Professor Clayton's wife. She stood at a lectern and read in a clear voice which was given body by microphones set on either side. She looked in her way as remarkable as Lady Fellowes.

In the body of the auditorium were perhaps six or seven hundred men and a few dozen women; if Roger had a surprise it was that so many of these 'old fossils' were in their twenties and thirties, the number of white and bald heads was comparatively small.

Each one in the audience was listening, enthralled.

". . . of the significance of what I have found I have no doubt at all; it is indeed possible that we have found the origins of man on the Australian continent which in the past has been so comparatively barren for our purposes. It is indeed possible that we have found what *vox populi* calls 'the missing link'—the missing link, that is, in the evolution of *homo sapiens*."

Rosamund Clayton paused.

Roger saw a battery of men and a few women in a section of the auditorium with a huge PRESS sign hanging over it; they were writing furiously. Every newspaper would carry this as a headline, many tonight, the rest tomorrow. He picked out plump Tweed, of the *Globe*. Well, that was hardly surprising.

Rosamund Clayton took a sip of water from a glass by her side, and then began to read her husband's paper again:

"Many of you will wonder why, since I was convinced that I had made a discovery of such importance, I did not immediately inform my colleagues—your good selves—and why I did not ask that a full scale exploration be put in hand; one of the greatest if not the greatest anthropological excavations in history. For if I am right, and I am convinced that I am, then an area some five miles by eleven miles, fifty-five square miles, will have to be exhaustively examined. It is my belief that within this area there appears to lie, buried deep beneath the red earth, a city many millions of years old, in which are the remains of a civilisation created by the first fully developed man.

"But I was not the first light upon this—to me—sacred spot," Rosamund read; and for the first time, her voice faltered; she sipped more water before going on, still in a husky voice: "Another kind of exploration had taken place in a series of caves on the site. There was, it appears, an enormous discovery of diamonds. There was, also, uranium ore of greatest purity. There was gold, one of the most extensive discoveries in the history of Australia, one of the great gold-producing lands of the world. And I discovered that this land had been acquired—bought—by a syndicate which was about to exploit it commercially, first by blasting operations which would destroy the evidence of the prehistoric past so precious to those who love mankind."

It seemed that every man and woman in the audience drew a deep breath; of horror or dismay. And, sensing this, Rosamund Clayton paused, looking up at the assembled faces before her; the young and the old; the white and the black; the red and the yellow. Most were in western style dress but here and there a splash of colour showed an African chief, in robes; one North American Indian wore a feathered head-dress; one Japanese woman, her kimono. Into the pause a man called in a high-pitched voice:

"No! It is a crime! It must never happen!"

"No!" another yelled.

"No! No! No! No!" came from all corners of the great room.

Slowly, Rosamund held up her hands, palms outwards; and the protests died away, so she began to read again with even greater clarity, as if she knew that each word would matter to all those who listened.

"First," she repeated, "by blasting operations which would destroy the precious evidence, and next by mining and drilling for the diamonds and the precious metals without regard for the past."

"It is a crime!" a man burst out.

"So, I came to an understanding with the members of the syndicate, whose names are listed as an appendix to this paper. I agreed to give them twelve months, which expires today, in which to make alternative plans; to mine from other directions and not to blast; to protect man's heritage while permitting the benefits for today's civilisations. They agreed to this. I made it clear to them that I would, in this paper to you, my honoured colleagues, reveal *all* the facts, including the exact site of the discoveries. I told them I was certain that you would also agree to what I had agreed—to share this great discovery, which may well prove the most important in mankind's history."

Rosamund paused again. This time there was no interruption; only what appeared to be a great sigh from all parts of the room. A moment later Roger saw the plump reporter from the *Globe* get up and move away from the *Press* section. He was apologising as he moved, reached a gangway and headed quickly for the main doors. As he approached he saw Roger, and said in a whisper:

"Must catch the next edition. I'll be back." He put his right hand to his pocket and pulled at a handkerchief, but before he got it free Roger's fingers tightened like a clamp round his wrist. He tugged. "What the hell are *you* doing?"

"Stopping you," Roger said.

Tweed swung his free arm in a vicious blow, and kicked at the same time. Roger held on to the wrist, keeping the man's hand in his own pocket. The security man and the policeman came hurrying, and Roger whispered:

"Get him out!"

The security man grabbed the other's free arm and pushed it up behind his back in a hammerlock, Roger twisted the wrist in his grip until Tweed gasped with pain and let Roger pull the hand free of the pocket. Roger dipped into the pocket and found what looked like a tennis ball, but made of cement.

"Be careful with that!" gasped Tweed. "Be careful! It will blow the whole place to pieces!"

"Whereas you wanted to blow the crowd in there to pieces," Roger said, savagely. He left Tweed to the others, and held the 'ball' gingerly as they went out into the street. More police were there and his car was still double-parked; but everything was quiet. Tweed looked desperately up and down; he was trembling all over.

"Expecting someone?" asked Roger. "Expecting a bodyguard of Hokki Braves to get you away safely?" Tweed looked dumbfounded, as Roger went on: "Most Hokkis which appeared on the streets today were picked up, and their drivers held," he stated. "None was allowed near here. You've been on your own all the time, Tweed. Or should I call you by the name your partner in all this calls you: Higginbottom."

"My God!" gasped Tweed. "Kevin's talked!"

"Kevin didn't get far away, but he hasn't talked yet," Roger said. "Both of you will before you're through."

He was standing with the 'ball' in his hand and Tweed looking at him helplessly when one of the detectives from the street came up, and said:

"Excuse me, Mr. West, but there's an urgent call for you, from the Yard."

"Tell *Information* I'm on my way," Roger said. "And tell them to send a bomb disposal unit to this place, quickly. They'll find this little beauty contains enough explosive to wreck the whole building and probably set it on fire. Better make a nest for it," he added. "Somewhere it can't fall."

One of the detectives took off his jacket and folded it with

180

great care, putting it on the ground close to the wall before Roger placed the 'ball' on it.

Then he stood back.

"One of you handcuff yourself to this man," he ordered, "and ride in the back of my car."

21

Confession

"You mean, you deliberately stayed away despite the call out for you?" Frobisher demanded in a harsh, angry voice. "This really is going too far even for a senior officer."

Coppell growled: "I agree. Did you, West?"

"Yes," admitted Roger. "I saw no alternative."

"Why the hell—" began Coppell.

"Explanations can hardly justify such defiance," Frobisher said coldly.

"I think they can, sir," Roger replied. "I think saving the lives of over seven hundred men and women has priority over obedience to instructions or regulations."

"What do you mean?" growled Coppell.

"Yes indeed: what do you mean?" demanded Frobisher, with less iciness in his voice. "I find it hard to believe you can justify such an extravagant statement."

Roger, standing in Coppell's room, while the other two sat and looked challengingly up at him, held himself very still for a moment, then moved to a chair and sat down. Perhaps the pallor which suddenly spread over his face stopped the others from making immediate comment. Coppell moved downwards to the right of his desk, took out a bottle of whisky and a glass, splashed in a little whisky and held it out to Roger, who took it with unsteady fingers.

"Thank you, sir." He gulped down half the drink, and then

closed his eyes. He could feel the spirit coursing through his veins, and kept quiet for a moment, then began to talk with his eyes half-closed.

"It was obvious from the beginning that this was a short-term affair," he said. "Clayton, Hubert Fellowes, his wife, Ida Spray and even I had to be kept out of action for a while—while some crime was committed. If we were killed incidentally, that didn't matter. So we had to find a short term objective. It was staring at me all the time but I didn't see it until the last moment. Clayton was attacked to prevent him from reading his paper to the Anthropological Conference, not because he came to me. He was blackmailed at that particular time to keep him away from the Conference. When that didn't work, he was attacked. And as a last resort they were prepared to blow up the whole Conference."

"Ida Spray could have known what Clayton was going to say; so could Rosamund Clayton," went on Roger. "So, through Ida, could Kevin Spray.

"That was one aspect of the case. The other were the actual suicides. When the motives didn't stand up, I kept looking for others. It was my sergeant, Venables, who really put me on the track; all three had been in Australia earlier this year. So had Clayton."

Coppell said: "I can follow you so far."

"We then come to the problem with the Hokki Braves—mostly a harmless motor-cycling group with a few bad ones mixed in. Kevin Spray was a Brave, so was his unseen and to us unknown friend, called Higginbottom. The bad ones were used to try to put me out of action and the police right off the scent. That much was obvious," he went on, and paused to sip more whisky. "But what was the real purpose? It had to be something in common between the three who committed suicide and Clayton—common knowledge, surely. Something short term: the Conference at the Museum Halls was a short-term affair. Once I put those two together my mind really began to work but there was no proof, sir. I could have the earlier potential victims such as Lady Fellowes and Mrs. Clayton watched, I could have an extra guard at the Halls, I could ask for all the Hokki cyclists to be held. What I couldn't do was to say for certain that disaster threatened the Conference. The Old Fossils," he added, almost to himself.

"But *why* should it?" demanded Coppell.

"You are in the same position as I am now, sir," Roger said: "You have my word, I had my convictions but not an explanation. I ran through everything I knew about the case time and time again, and came up with (a) there was going to be trouble at the Conference when Mrs. Clayton read her husband's paper, (b) the Chairman and other Old Fossils knew it was going to be a hot potato—I couldn't get a word out of them, (c) danger would probably come from the inside, and that meant a delegate or someone who could get into the Halls—and their security arrangements were nearly foolproof. There were only two ways a non-delegate could get into that meeting place without being suspected: one was as a policeman or security officer, and I had them checked; the other was as a newspaperman.

"This time, it was a newspaperman. I recognised—"

The telephone bell rang on Coppell's desk. He muttered something under his breath about 'told her to hold all calls', and snatched up the receiver. "I'm busy, I—eh? . . . *What's* that? . . . My God! . . . Yes, I'll tell him." He rang off; and now his face was pale and his voice very husky. "That was the lieutenant in charge of the bomb disposal unit you sent for, West. The bomb at the Halls contained enough high-explosive and incendiary matter to have burned down the Halls and probably the whole block, including the museum."

Roger said heavily: "Ten seconds later, and he would have thrown it."

"Who would have thrown it?" demanded Frobisher.

"The newspaperman who proved to be the only practical suspect," Roger answered. "A man named Tweed, of the *Globe*.

He may not be on their regular staff, may be a freelance. It turned out that he has an *alias:* Higginbottom. He is a Hokki Brave and a close friend of Kevin Spray. I have very little doubt that Ida Spray told her son about this discovery, he told Higginbottom *alias* Tweed, and between them they planned the takeover."

"Takeover of what?" roared Coppell.

"Oh, I'm sorry, sir," Roger said. "This whole case has been upside down from the start. A syndicate consisting of a banker—Sir Jeremy Gooden—a highly-placed civil servant—Sir Douglas Fellowes—and a renowned pilot used to flying solo over desert, made a discovery of fantastic commercial value in the dead heart of Australia. They made the mistake of trying to develop this on their own—Fellowes using his authority as a highly-placed Civil Servant to help buy the land for next to nothing; Gooden, embezzling money to keep the scheme going; Aker, flying out samples of diamonds, gold and uranium ore. All went well until Clayton, who had explored caves in the area years ago, made another discovery which he thinks is a kind of city of missing links.

"Clayton did a deal with the syndicate, but didn't reckon with his son, who hated him anyway, and Higginbottom taking over. To work their ill-gotten gains effectively, Kevin Spray and Higginbotton *alias* Tweed had to keep the discovery a secret. Clayton was going to tell the Conference, so the so-called secret would have become common knowledge. The others who had made a deal to give Clayton and his Old Fossils time to dig and research, also had to go. So did Hubert Fellowes, in whom his father had confided."

"You mean they would have killed indiscriminately," breathed Frobisher.

"I think you fail to realise, sir, how many young people today really do think that anyone over thirty is useless and should be put away," Roger said. "I haven't any doubt that Kevin Spray and Higginbottom-Tweed are two of them. They saw a fortune for the taking. They used the rotten apples among their club members to help—no doubt offering free drugs. They are two *very* evil young men."

"Oh, I hate him," Kevin Spray said, viciously. "I don't owe him a bloody thing. The whole generation ought to be wiped out. But I tried to fix him with blackmail, if he'd fallen for that there would have been no need for the attack."

"There are too many old people in the world," stated Tweed coldly. "All they do is hold up progress. The world belongs to the young. I'm only sorry we didn't kill Clayton."

"Yes," breathed Ida Spray. "I'd forgotten, but I did tell Kevin that Richard was going to read his paper to the Conference. That—that must be what started it all."

"Not started," Roger said. "It triggered off the final explosion, that's all."

He left her, and went to his office, where there was a note saying: *"See me—Commander C."* Venables tapped and came in, a happy young man, with good news. Both Professor Clayton and Hubert Fellowes would recover. The round-up of Hokki Braves had brought the names of fifty-one who had been involved in the Battle of Bell Street, and all had been brought from the clubs which had been unsuccessfully raided; all were drug addicts.

"Oh, and Mr. Coppell would like to see you, sir."

With Coppell was the Assistant Commissioner, still somewhat aloof, not a man whom Roger felt he would ever get to know well. But at least he had good qualities, for he said:

"I wanted to tell you, Superintendent, that my attitude towards you was due to information that you yourself were much better informed than appeared easily explainable. My information came from a highly-respected newspaper owner, who freely admits that *his* information came from the man Tweed. Further, we had some reason to suspect the extensive purchase of land by Fellowes, and you appeared in very close touch with his widow. It seemed safer to take no chances with you. I must apologise."

"No need, sir," Roger said. "But thank you."

"Handsome," Coppell put in, "I want you to look after the cases against Tweed and Spray. Keep in close touch with the Public Prosecutor's office and take as much time as you need."

"Thank you," Roger said. He was never too happy about the clearing up of a case but this time it was inevitable. "May I make a recommendation, sir?"

"What about?"

"Detective Sergeant Venables will make a very good Detective Inspector."

"I'll see to it," Coppell said. For once, all he seemed to want was to please Roger.

Roger went back to the office, decided not to tell Venables yet, for the promotion might take some time. He was going through reports on the case when the telephone bell rang, and to his surprise the operator said:

"Professor Clayton is on the line, sir."

"Put him through," said Roger, and a moment later: *"Very glad to hear you, sir."*

"I've a telephone at my bedside," Clayton told Roger, "and I wanted my first call to be to you, Superintendent. I hope you will take my personal thanks and gratitude for granted. I am truly, deeply grateful, for you saved the life of my wife. I am also grateful beyond words that you have been so considerate of Mrs. Spray. You will understand that I feel I *must* do all I can to defend our son, won't you?"

"Of course, sir."

"Thank you. The International Convention of Anthropologists is, I understand, going to offer you an associate fellowship, and I do hope you can see your way to accept. They can think of no more effective method of expressing their deep gratitude." Before Roger could answer, Clayton went on: "An expedition is already being organised to explore the discovery I was fortunate enough to make, and I shall join this as soon as I am well enough. We shall of course co-operate as far as practicable with commercial and government interests."

"I'm sure you will," Roger said. "I am very glad."

"And finally, my wife—who is here with me—would like to add her thanks," Clayton said. "Here you are, darling," he added in a voice which faded.

A moment later, Rosamund's voice sounded, but Roger did not take in all she said. She must have heard the 'our son' earlier; she must know about Ida Spray.

Later she was with Clayton in this time of trial and of triumph.